"Haven't I made it clear that I have no interest in you?"

His smile was warm and amused. "Very clear. But the pursuit is part of the attraction."

"And you intend to use my son to get through to me?"

"No, it's hardly fair."

"But he needs a man in his life—that's what you're still trying to tell me?" she asked bitterly. "I thank you for your offer and I won't disappoint Daniel now, but please don't put any other tempting offers in his way."

"You're a courageous woman, Hannah Carpenter, determined and independent, and very, very attractive." Before she could anticipate his actions, he lowered his head and dropped a light kiss on her mouth.

MARGARET MAYO began writing quite by chance when the engineering company she worked for wasn't very busy and she found herself with time on her hands. Today, with more than thirty romance novels to her credit, she admits that writing governs her life to a large extent. When she and her husband holiday—Cornwall is their favorite spot—Margaret always has a notebook and camera on hand and is constantly looking for fresh ideas. She lives in the countryside near Stafford, England.

Books by Margaret Mayo

HARLEQUIN PRESENTS
963—PASSIONATE VENGEANCE
1045—SAVAGE AFFAIR
1108—A PAINFUL LOVING
1187—PRISONER OF THE MIND
1525—A FIERY ENCOUNTER

HARLEQUIN ROMANCE
2937—FEELINGS
2955—UNEXPECTED INHERITANCE
3003—BITTERSWEET PURSUIT
3029—CONFLICT
3155—TRAPPED
3190—AN IMPOSSIBLE SITUATION

MARGARET MAYO

Stormy Relationship

Harlequin Books

TORONTO • NEW YORK • LONDON
AMSTERDAM • PARIS • SYDNEY • HAMBURG
STOCKHOLM • ATHENS • TOKYO • MILAN
MADRID • WARSAW • BUDAPEST • AUCKLAND

ISBN 0-373-11652-7

STORMY RELATIONSHIP

Copyright © 1991 by Margaret Mayo.

This edition published by arrangement with Harlequin Enterprises B. V.

Printed in U.S.A.

CHAPTER ONE

'THAT man is impossible! He's not only impossible, he's an arrogant swine, and I don't know why I stick it here!'

Hannah grinned at Christine's flushed face. 'You stick it because you know you wouldn't get a better wage anywhere else. I wish I earned as much as you.'

'Happiness is more important than money,' Christine announced patronisingly. 'I'm looking in the paper tonight for another job.' And, so saying, she flounced out of the office.

Happiness wasn't always more important than money, thought Hannah, not when there was never enough to make ends meet. What the employment agency paid her was a pittance compared with the salaries Jordan Quest paid his staff. She had found that much out in the few weeks she had worked as his temporary secretary. If only she could manage a full-time job!

'Mrs Carpenter!'

The command was imperious—as always! She quickly gathered her wits, together with her notebook and pencil, and entered Jordan Quest's office. He was tall, over six feet, and dark, his face strongly angular, every feature strikingly dominant—deep-set eyes that were ferociously black, thick brows bridging them, a harshly defined mouth, a chiselled jaw, a body that was honed to physical perfection.

The toughness was further evident in his imperious bearing, his commanding attitude, and the fierce power that emanated from every pore in his body. He was not

a man to cross, as most of his employees had found out
to their cost. On the other hand, he was, to give him his
due, exceedingly fair, and more than generous where
wages were concerned.

For the next half-hour he barked instructions at
Hannah, giving her no time to query anything he said,
and lord help her if she did not get everything right! Tell
Jones I want to see him immediately, make sure that
letter to Bridger gets sent out today, book me a room at
the Royal for Wednesday night, and so on and so on.

In the two years Hannah had been with the agency
she had worked for a few difficult people, but Jordan
Quest was, without a doubt, more demanding, more
exacting and more impossible than anyone else. She
knew, though, that if she did not want him to send a
bad report to the agency and maybe jeopardise her job,
then she had to stand up to him. So she ignored his bad
moods to the best of her ability, defended herself if she
felt she was in the right, and got on with her job. She
was quick and accurate and made sure he never had cause
for complaint.

She half suspected that he never even saw her; she was
a human machine conditioned to do a job, and if the
job was well done that was all he cared. She was the
latest in a long line of temporary secretaries and had
lasted longer than most, some only managing a few
hours. Hannah had been with him for a few weeks.

Returning to her office to carry out his requests, she
soon heard his voice raised in argument with Andrew
Jones. Andrew was his costings director and had been
with the company since its conception. He was a brilliant
man but lacked his employer's dedication, and Jordan
Quest came down on people like a ton of bricks if they

fell below the standards he set, the ones he adhered to himself.

He worked hard and long hours, and demanded the same of everyone else. He was no respecter of family life. He expected his employees to put their jobs first and could not understand when they complained. As far as he was concerned, Quest Electronics was *the* most important thing in his life, so why wasn't it in theirs? Why didn't they give it the same consideration?

Andrew Jones' face was a fiery red as he made his exit, and Hannah felt sorry for him. The next second Jordan Quest himself erupted into her office like a whirlwind. 'Mrs Carpenter, I urgently need you to work over. In fact, I need you full time. I want you to be my permanent secretary. No one else can cope with the job like you do. I'll make it worth your while. I've already had a word with your agency and they're prepared to let you go.'

Hannah looked at him for a moment in open-mouthed, wide-eyed astonishment, totally taken aback by his suggestion. 'I'm sorry, Mr Quest, it's impossible,' she said. And she really was sorry; it was a wonderful opportunity, the money was exactly what she needed. And she liked the job despite his overbearing attitude. Hard work was her panacea, in fact. It had been for the last two years.

'What?' His expression suggested he could not believe that she was turning down such a good offer, black eyes blazing, brows drawn into a furious frown. 'I'll double the salary you're getting now, triple it even. I need you, Mrs Carpenter, you're the only one who can put up with my black moods.'

Her lips quirked. At least he knew his faults. 'All I do is ignore them and get on with my job, Mr Quest.'

'Which you do excellently. I can't fault your work. As you know, my standards are high. I pay for efficiency and I expect it. Name your salary.' He rested his hands on the edge of her desk, leaning forward so that his eyes were on a level with hers, fiercely demanding her submission.

For the first time Hannah felt the full impact of this man to whom power meant everything, felt faint alarm at his insistence, his confidence that she would accept, but she also felt an irrational stirring of her senses, because, despite his inflexibility, he was a sensual male animal. But still she shook her head, and his brow grew even blacker.

'What is this, a conspiracy against me?' he raged. 'I've just asked Jones to work late and he refuses. I've an important meeting in the morning for which I need very precise figures and a critical document typing. You're the only person who can do it neatly and accurately in so short a time.'

'In that case, Mr Quest, you shouldn't have left it until the last minute,' she told him calmly. 'I'm sorry, I can't work late.' He had compelling eyes, she thought. Up until now she had not really looked into them. Now she noticed that they weren't black at all but a very dark brown ringed with black, but as hard as polished jet, and his long sweeping lashes were quite extraordinary on a man, but in no way did they soften his image.

'I don't believe this!' His tone was harshly condemning. 'What's so important that you have to leave at three on the dot every day? Every self-respecting secretary works whatever hours her boss needs her.'

'The agency are my employers, Mr Quest,' she reminded him. 'Doing temporary work is the only way I can dictate my own hours. Half-past nine until three is perfect. And I never work at all during school holidays.'

'You have children?' He jerked away from the desk, a scowl appearing. This was obviously something that had never occurred to him—and why should it have? She was a temporary secretary, nothing more, there had been no need for him to ask personal questions.

Hannah smiled and nodded, her blue eyes soft with love and pride. 'I have an eight-year-old son, and I always take him to school and fetch him back.'

He shook his head as if unable to accept that something as simple as a child was coming between him and the work he needed doing. 'You have no neighbours who could do this for you? Who could look after him while you're at work? Isn't that what most mothers do?'

'It's not what I do.' She could have asked Yvonne, she supposed, but she hated the thought of entrusting Daniel to anyone else. Roger had been taken from her, and if anything happened to Daniel life would not be worth living. He was her whole life. He was all she had left of the man she had loved so dearly.

'It's vital I get this document typed.' The scowl persisted. He was a man who did not take kindly to having his plans thwarted.

Hannah glanced at her watch. 'If I start now I might get it finished before three,' she said.

He snorted testily, 'That's the trouble, I haven't yet got all the information.' He paced the room and, watching him, seeing his animal grace, the lithe movements of his long muscular legs, Hannah yet again acknowledged his sexuality, yet did not feel any response to it. It had been this way since her husband's accident. Roger had been her whole world and she was not interested in other men. Her friends all said that she ought to start looking around, and were continually trying to fix her up with a date, but she wanted nothing to do with their matchmaking.

'I have it.' He abruptly stopped his pacing, his brown eyes fixed intently on her blue ones. 'You fetch your son here. He can sit in the corner and draw, or do whatever he wants as long as he's quiet about it, while you get on with my work. And then tomorrow we'll discuss again your working for me on a permanent basis.'

He was so convinced that he had found the perfect solution, that she would agree without demur, that Hannah almost rejected his suggestion. And she was actually so long in answering that he added impatiently, 'I'll obviously pay you for the extra hours, over and above whatever you get from the agency.'

'OK, I'll fetch Daniel,' she said, the thought of the extra money making it all worth while, 'but there's no way I'll become your permanent secretary unless I can dictate my own hours.'

He gave a snort of anger and looked at her with cold contempt. Hannah had lost weight during the last two years, and there were shadows beneath her eyes due to too many sleepless nights. Yet she was still pretty. Her face had a good bone-structure and her wide blue eyes had thick black lashes which needed no artificial aids to enhance them. In fact she rarely wore make-up. Her brown hair was short and naturally curly and she cut it herself whenever it got too long. There was never enough money for visits to the hairdresser. Almost every penny she earned was spent on food, and clothes for Daniel. He wore shoes out as though they were made of paper, and he was forever coming home with the knees out of his trousers.

He missed his father as much as Hannah did, and she wished he had another brother or sister to play with. They had dearly wanted more children, but none had come along, and they had thought they had plenty of time. Neither of them had realised how precious life was.

'Is it the child's father who's so much against you leaving him?' The words were thrust at her with savage intolerance.

Hannah closed her eyes, a vision of Roger appearing on the backs of her lids, handsome and blond. He had meant everything to her. No one could ever replace him.

'Mrs Carpenter, is something wrong?'

She suddenly realised that the seconds were ticking away and he was waiting edgily for her answer. 'I'm sorry, my mind flew back. I'm a widow, Mr Quest. I lost my husband two years ago.'

It was his turn to pause, fleeting surprise in his eyes, but he did not offer his condolences. 'In that case you need a job more than ever—a permanent job to give you security. Go and fetch your son now, and then think about it.'

Hannah did not see that there was anything to think about. The high salary he offered was like a dream come true. She desperately needed more money, but to leave Daniel with someone else? It went against all her principles.

Daniel was intrigued and excited when he discovered that he was going to the place where his mother worked, and even though she warned him that he would have to sit still and keep very quiet he shrugged it off easily. 'Of course I'll be quiet, Mummy. I can write and pretend I'm working just like you.'

What Hannah had not realised was exactly how late Jordan Quest would keep her. The proposed contract was sixty pages long and he still wanted alterations made after it was finished. Her work was made easier with a word processor, but even so it was time-consuming, and Daniel began to get restless. 'When are we going, Mummy?' he kept asking. 'I'm hungry, I want my tea.'

Apart from giving him a cursory glance Jordan Quest had ignored her son, and Hannah guessed he hadn't much time or patience for little boys. Aged thirty-five and not married, he had a reputation for being a womaniser. His present girlfriend had called into the office not long after Hannah had begun working there, ostensibly to see Jordan, but Hannah had a feeling it was to vet her—to make sure she wasn't a potential rival. She was beautiful and blonde and brittle, and Hannah had not been able to see what he saw in her.

Now, Jordan heard Daniel complaining, and before Hannah knew it a sandwich and a cake appeared on the table in front of the child, together with a glass of iced orange juice. So he wasn't entirely a hard-hearted monster, she thought, surprised by the gesture.

Everyone else had gone home by the time they were finished, and they walked out of the building together. 'Where's your car?' asked Jordan, looking round the empty car park—empty, that was, except for his low-slung red Ferrari.

'I don't have a car,' she said.

He frowned. 'You don't drive?'

'Yes, but after my husband died the car was too expensive to run, and I've never bothered with another.' She and Danny walked everywhere, taking a bus only when it was absolutely necessary. She had to count every single penny. The rent on the flat was horrendous, but it was all she had been able to get when she was forced to give up the house.

'Then I'll give you a lift.' He held up an imperious hand when she automatically began to protest. 'It's the very least I can do.'

Daniel's eyes grew wide with excitement when he realised what was happening, and he raced across to the car, standing beside it and admiring its long smooth lines and gleaming paintwork.

'It's a Ferrari Mondial,' announced Jordan, noticing Daniel's interest as he unlocked the door and held it open.

Amazing Hannah, because he was usually very shy with strangers, Daniel scrambled on to the rich leather seat without waiting to be told.

'Into the back, young man,' urged Jordan. 'Make room for your mother.'

Obediently he climbed over and sat down, one hand on each of the front seats, peering with interest at the dials on the dashboard.

'Sit back and fasten your belt,' commanded Hannah as she got in too. Daniel obeyed reluctantly.

As they pulled away she felt the car close in around her. She had never been locked into such a tiny space with Jordan Quest, and she felt the charisma that drew so many girls to him, felt his overt sexuality, and knew that if she weren't still in love with Roger she could easily have found herself attracted.

Fortunately the journey was short, Jordan following her instructions to the narrow back street where they lived in a converted Victorian house which fronted straight on to the street.

'Is this it?' he frowned.

She could almost see his nose turning up in disgust. 'I'm afraid so.'

'You live in a flat?'

Hannah nodded.

'Where does the boy play?'

'I take him to the park.'

'Heavens! Why have you never moved into a house with a garden? This is no sort of environment to bring up a child!'

Hannah's chin jutted. 'Not that I think it's any business of yours, Mr Quest, but we had used to live in a cottage. My husband worked on a farm. However, it went with his job and I had to get out after he died. This is all I can afford.'

He frowned. 'But surely there was insurance money that would have bought you a small place?'

She shook her head. 'I'm afraid not. For years we talked about taking out life insurance, but we kept putting it off—until in the end it was too late. Somehow you never think that you're going to die at that age.'

Money had been short even in those days. As a farmhand Roger hadn't earned a very high wage, and he had insisted when Daniel was born that she give up her job and stay at home to look after him. He felt strongly about mothers going out to work. They had grown all their own vegetables and been more or less self-sufficient, so it had been no real problem—until she was left to bring Daniel up alone! After a refresher course in secretarial skills she had taken a job with the agency and just about managed to keep their heads above water. But it was a real struggle at times.

'I see.' Jordan's eyes were thoughtful. 'All the more reason for you to take the job I'm offering. I'll see you in the morning, Mrs Carpenter.'

The instant Hannah arrived the following day Jordan called her into his office and bade her sit down. He walked around his desk and leaned back against the edge of it, his eyes slowly appraising her slender figure in her tailored grey suit. It was her one and only suit and was almost her office uniform. She rang the changes each day with a different blouse.

It was as though he was seeing her, really seeing her, for the first time, and she felt slightly uncomfortable, even though there was nothing in his expression to show that he was interested in her in any other way than as a competent secretary. Yet even so...

When he spoke he startled her. 'Well, Mrs Carpenter, what is your decision?'

Hannah had thought long and hard last night about his proposal. Yvonne Howard in the flat below had offered some time ago to look after Daniel if she ever needed anyone, and Hannah had gone down to see her when Daniel was asleep. Mrs Howard had said straight away that she would be delighted and that Hannah would be a fool to turn down such a generous offer. The only thing was that from five to seven each day she did some voluntary work for the Samaritans, and could Hannah be home by a quarter to five?

Yvonne was much older than Hannah, a widow too, but with no children. She had been pregnant when her husband had died, and the shock of it had caused her to lose the baby. This was why she took so much interest in Daniel. Her son would have been roughly the same age.

Still Hannah hesitated to accept. It was a big step. She had never left Daniel in anyone's care, except her own parents, of course, but they now lived in Scotland and she only saw them when she took Daniel up during the school holidays. They had wanted her to move up there when Roger died, but she had thought it would be too much of an upheaval for Daniel.

'I can't see what your problem is.' The irritation of yesterday was back in Jordan Quest's voice.

'It's not an easy decision,' she said. 'I've never left Daniel with anyone before. He might not be happy. I——'

'OK, OK, name your hours.' Harsh impatience came out on a sigh.

She thought swiftly. 'I'll work from half-past nine till half-past four.' That way she could still take Daniel to school. It wouldn't be so much of an inconvenience for Mrs Howard.

'And during school holidays?'

'The same,' she acknowledged, and thought she saw relief in his eyes. 'But if Daniel's ill then I shall want to be at home with him.'

He nodded. 'Of course.'

His easy acceptance amazed her, made her realise how desperate he was for her services. But goodness, how useful the extra money would be! It would mean the difference between living on the breadline and living in relative comfort. She had never been so short of money in her life. Sometimes she lay awake worrying that she would not have enough to pay the bills. And Daniel couldn't understand why he never had expensive toys the same as his friends. A sense of relief came over her.

Jordan moved briskly back behind his desk. 'Now that's settled I'd like some coffee before I go to my meeting. Oh, and Mrs Carpenter, I'd like you to come too and take some notes.'

It was the first time he had asked her to do anything like this, but she supposed that now she was his official secretary she would be required to do all sorts of things that he had not entrusted her with before.

The morning fled, and because Hannah had not fixed up anything definite with Yvonne she went home at lunchtime to ask her if she would fetch Daniel from school. The older woman was delighted Hannah had taken the job and told her not to worry about a thing.

At half-past four Jordan came into Hannah's office. 'I'd like this typed out immediately and faxed through to Temple Products.' He did not seem to notice that her desk was cleared and her bag in her hand.

'I'm sorry, Mr Quest, but I'm leaving now,' she said firmly.

He frowned harshly and shot back his cuff to look at his gold Rolex watch, then swore beneath his breath. 'This won't take a minute, and it is important.'

'I'm sorry,' she said again more firmly. 'But my son is also important. You agreed I could leave at half-past four, and it's——'

'Mrs Carpenter,' he butted in peremptorily, 'I wouldn't ask if it weren't urgent.'

'And how often are you going to have something urgent when it's time for me to go home?' Hannah countered, looking up at him from her five feet four. Everything was urgent as far as he was concerned. 'This job isn't going to work, I can see that now. I was a fool to think I could manage the extra hours. You'd better find yourself someone else with no commitments, someone who can work all the hours God made just to suit you.'

Jordan snorted his impatience. 'I don't want anyone else, you're the best secretary I've ever had.'

'Then if you don't want to lose me you'll have to let me go now. A neighbour is looking after Daniel, but

she goes out at a quarter to five. I must be there by
then.'

His nostrils dilated as he looked at her. He seemed in
the most towering rage, but she was not frightened of
him. All he could do was tell her the job was no longer
hers. And then to her amazement he smiled. 'No one
else defies me the way you do, Mrs Carpenter—Hannah,
isn't it? You're a gutsy lady, and I admire you for that.
We'll reach a compromise. You do my letter and I'll drive
you home.'

Opening her mouth to reject his suggestion, Hannah
caught the look in his eyes and changed her mind. Despite the fact that his mouth smiled, his eyes were hard.
He intended getting that letter done at whatever cost,
and all she was doing was wasting precious time arguing.

But in his Ferrari, the letter safely faxed to the cus-
tomer, his mood changed. He glanced at her often, an
altogether different expression on his face from the one
she saw at the office. It was as if, for once, he had pushed
work behind him and was concentrating on her alone,
showing some interest in her other than as a human machine. Maybe it was all in her mind, but she had not
forgotten the way he looked at her this morning, and
her skin prickled with an unaccustomed warmth.

Nothing like this had happened when he thought she
was a respectable married lady, it was only since he had
learned that she was a widow that he had looked at her
with even a degree of humanity. And she could not help
thinking of his reputation as a womaniser. Did he think
she might be easy game? A lot of men assumed that
widows missed having a man in their bed. Was this what
Jordan Quest thought? She would certainly never stand
any nonsense in that direction. If he tried anything she
would nip it swiftly in the bud, let him know without

any doubt that she was not interested. She was interested in no other man, she still loved Roger. And yet—his raw sexuality was something that could not be ignored. It was impossible to draw breath without swallowing him in. It had been very unwise to accept this lift.

She had not realised her mouth had tightened until he said, 'You're not happy with the situation?'

'What situation?' she frowned, feeling faint colour in her cheeks. Surely he hadn't read her thoughts?

'Working longer hours? It worries you leaving your son?'

Relief flooded through her. 'Yes, it worries me,' she admitted. 'I think it would worry any caring mother. But I've every confidence in Mrs Howard, even though she's never looked after Daniel before.' Thank goodness Jordan had not guessed that her thoughts were of a much more personal nature!

The journey was short, and Mrs Howard was with Daniel on the front step looking out for her. She looked surprised to see Hannah arriving in an expensive red sports car, but Daniel recognised it and ran forward eagerly.

'I'm sorry, Yvonne,' said Hannah, scrambling out and grimacing ruefully. 'Mr Quest had an urgent letter. I hope I haven't made you late?'

Jordan Quest unfolded himself from the car too and smiled warmly at the older woman. 'It was entirely my fault—I take all the blame. Perhaps I can give you a lift?'

Yvonne Howard's cheeks grew rosy under the warmth of his smile, and Hannah could see that here was another woman falling prey to his charm. Her lips tugged down in disapproval and she turned away—in time to see Daniel crawling into Jordan's car. 'Danny, come out of there at once!' she scolded, embarrassed that he was being so naughty.

Jordan glanced around. 'Leave the boy, he's enjoying himself.' And then he turned his attention back to Yvonne. They continued to talk quietly for a few minutes before Yvonne said she really must go. 'I'll pick Daniel up from school tomorrow, Hannah,' she said. 'Don't worry about him.'

By this time Daniel was sitting behind the steering-wheel pretending to drive, and Hannah felt sure that Jordan would tell him off. To her surprise all he did was smile and lift Daniel out. 'One day, young man, I'll take you out in it, if you're very good,' he said.

'Really?' Daniel's blue eyes shone. 'Did you hear that, Mummy? Mr Quest's going to take me out in his car!'

'And your mother too.' Jordan's eyes locked into Hannah's, and this time there was a definite warmth in them that could not be ignored.

CHAPTER TWO

WHEN Hannah went to the office the next morning she was consoled by the fact that Jordan Quest had reverted to the businesslike image she was used to and knew how to handle. Apart from a brief appraisal of her soft, feminine body in a blue cotton dress, he barked out his orders in a no-nonsense voice, and she might have imagined the deepening of his tone when he had intimated that he would like to take her out.

She had lain awake for a good part of the night thinking about him, about the way his attitude towards her seemed to be changing, about the way she responded to him against her will, and the fact that she wasn't the only girl to feel this way. The only difference between herself and other girls was that she intended to fight her feelings. She would not let him see how she felt—she had no intention of becoming another statistic, another in a long line of conquests! In any case, he wasn't her type. If, and it was a very big if, she ever got involved with a man again he would need to be someone like Roger, someone gentle and kind, someone who never raised their voice or tried to put her down.

She was more than a little surprised when Jordan came into her office at half-past four and offered to take her home again. 'That isn't necessary, Mr Quest, I have plenty of time today, and I'm sure you're far too busy,' she said.

He looked at her with that expression in his eyes that she had seen much too frequently lately, an interest in her other than professional. 'I think it's time you called me Jordan.' Again that low sensual timbre to his voice.

Hannah's chin tilted. 'I don't mean to be rude, *Mr* Quest, but I'd prefer to keep our relationship on a strictly business level.'

A flash of annoyance crossed his face, gone so swiftly she might have imagined it. A faint frown drew the thick brows together. 'As you wish—Hannah—but I'd still like to give you a lift.'

He said her name as no one else ever had, stretching the last syllable, giving it an almost foreign inflexion. She tried not to admit that she liked it. 'No, thank you— it's a nice day, I prefer to walk.' He had never before left the office this early unless he had business to attend to, and she knew it was his new-found interest in her that was the cause of it, but she was determined not to start something she might later regret.

'You intrigue me, do you know that, Hannah? You're so damned independent. Have you let no other man into your life since your husband died?'

'No,' she told him frankly. 'Nor do I intend to.'

'You're still in love with your husband, is that it?' He sounded as though he found this impossible to accept. 'You're not yet ready to start another relationship?'

'No, I'm not,' she admitted, her tone quietly steady. 'As a matter of fact I have no intention of ever getting married again.' No one could compare with Roger. When he'd died she had been completely devastated and had wanted to kill herself too. Daniel had kept her sane. She had forced herself to be cheerful in front of him, only crying her tears of grief when alone in bed at night. Now she had come to terms with it, but she wanted no one else. She had made her own little world and was happy. Happy enough. She would like a house with a garden, but that was all, and maybe even that would be possible now she was earning a good salary.

Jordan's rugged brows rose. 'That's a mistake, and a great pity as far as your son is concerned. Don't you think he could do with some male company, a father figure to guide him?'

Hannah shrugged. 'We have no problems in that respect.'

He looked at her steadily. 'I think *you* have a problem, one we should discuss some time.'

She let her breath out on a hiss of impatience. 'If I did have a problem, which I haven't, I assure you, you're the last person I'd talk it over with. We have nothing in common, Mr Quest, we know nothing at all about each other. What gives you the right to think you can help me?'

A muscle flicked in his jaw, showing that her outburst had displeased him, but his tone was perfectly even when he spoke. 'I'd like to think we could become friends.'

Her chin lifted. 'I don't think so. I know the type of friendship you're thinking of. Now, if you'll excuse me, I really must go.'

Her insinuation caused a further flash of anger, but to her surprise he crossed the room and opened the door. He was not letting her get away that easily, though. As she walked past him his hand caught her elbow. 'Don't freeze me out altogether, Hannah.' His voice was a low soft growl in her ear. 'It doesn't suit you, being an ice-maiden. You're far too beautiful and sensuous.'

Hannah felt her heart give an unsteady bump. It was the first time anyone had told her that. Even Roger, for all that he had loved her dearly, had never paid her compliments of that sort. Her cheeks felt warm as she left the building and hurried home.

Yvonne saw her coming and her door stood open. 'No lift from your handsome boss today?' She looked disappointed, and Hannah wondered if she ought to warn her that Jordan was a womaniser and not to be trusted.

Instead she gave a weak smile. 'He didn't have anything urgent to make me late. Has Danny been a good boy?'

'Of course I've been good,' said Daniel scornfully, appearing at Yvonne Howard's side. 'Where's Mr Quest? He promised me a ride in his car.'

'Mr Quest is a very busy man,' said Hannah. Her boss had certainly made a big impact on them! 'And I don't think you should rely on him keeping his word.'

'Why did he say it if he didn't mean it?' frowned her son. 'That's not right. You always tell me that——'

'That will do, Danny,' she cut in firmly. 'Let's go home now so that Mrs Howard can go to work.'

All evening Daniel kept talking about Jordan Quest and his car and the fact that he had promised him a ride, until Hannah felt like screaming and was glad when her son was in bed. What was it about the man that had created such an impression? On her too, if the truth were known, though she was less kindly disposed towards him than either Daniel or Yvonne. She knew him too well to be deceived by his surface charm.

An important board meeting the next day meant that Hannah was kept busy taking notes which Jordan then expected her to type out before she went home, as well as all the other letters and instructions he had dictated on to tape before she arrived. When four o'clock approached and she was nowhere near the end she knew it was an impossible task, and decided to tell Jordan

Quest now rather than wait until it was time for her to go home.

But before she reached his office her own door opened to admit the heavily perfumed Riva March. The blonde beauty threw a malevolent glance at Hannah. 'Just a minute, I want a word with you.'

Hannah showed her surprise, wondering what she had done to cause the girl to look at her like that. Riva was dressed in a scarlet figure-hugging dress, her fingertips dripping the same colour. She no doubt thought that she oozed sexuality, but as far as Hannah was concerned she made her feel sick. And she could not imagine for one minute what Jordan saw in her.

'I understand Jordan has given you the job of his permanent secretary?' Green eyes glittered hostilely. 'What did you do to bring off that little coup?'

'I don't know what you mean?' frowned Hannah.

'Come off it!' snapped Riva. 'I'm not that naïve. Every single secretary Jordan's had so far has wormed her way into his bed—don't tell me that's not what you've got in mind?'

Before Hannah could answer Riva went on, 'Things have changed now, Jordan belongs to me, so be warned, keep your scheming hands off him!'

About to tell her that she was welcome to him, Hannah was forestalled by Jordan himself coming into her office. 'Ah, I thought I heard voices. What are you doing here, Riva, at this time of day?'

Immediately the blonde was all smiles and sweetness. 'I was at a loose end, I thought you might take pity on me and finish early?' She swayed across the room and rested a hand proprietorially on his arm, lifting her face to press the pouting redness of her lips to his cheek. 'If I ring up you always say you're too busy, so I thought

I'd come in person.' She lifted a finger to rub delicately at the lipsticked outline her lips had left.

Hannah felt nauseated.

'Sweetheart, you know how impossible it is for me to get away.' He put his hands on either side of her face, seeming not to notice Hannah standing there. 'Why don't you go to my place? Mrs Braden will look after you. I'll be home as soon as I possibly can.'

It was obvious to Hannah that Riva was not pleased with this suggestion, and that her smile was as false as her ridiculously long eyelashes. 'If you promise not to be long, darling?'

'I'll do my best,' he said, and Hannah noted that he used the same toe-curling growl as he had when he told her she was beautiful the day before. What a two-faced swine he was! No doubt the instant Riva's back was turned the compliments would be back in her court.

He escorted the blonde to the door, murmuring something soft and low in her ear which caused her to give Hannah a sly triumphant smile over his shoulder. Grin all you like, she thought, you're welcome to him.

Once the girl had gone Hannah dived straight in. 'Mr Quest, I shan't have time to finish both the minutes and your letters. Which would you like me to do?'

An expected black scowl appeared on his brow; she knew how he hated leaving anything over until the next day. He glanced at his watch. 'There's no question about which you do. It's imperative I have everything on my desk before you leave this afternoon.'

'That's impossible, I'm afraid.' She fearlessly returned the coolness of his gaze.

'Ring Mrs Howard and tell her you'll be late,' he demanded imperiously.

'I can't do that,' Hannah protested. 'She does a job for the Samaritans. They rely on her to be punctual.'

He swore violently. 'It's obviously no good, you working these ridiculous hours. You'd better make some different arrangements as far as your son is concerned.'

Hannah drew herself up angrily. 'My son is more important to me than your job! If you're not happy with things the way they are then find yourself another secretary. I do my best to get your work done in the time I'm here. I'm sorry you're not satisfied.'

Jordan closed his eyes and swung angrily away. 'The question of being satisfied is not in dispute. These minutes are important. I need them for a meeting at nine o'clock in the morning.'

'So I'll do those and leave your letters.'

'But it's vital they're sent off today too.'

'Then get one of the other secretaries to do them.'

He snorted impatiently. 'And find half a dozen mistakes? Anyone would think I was an ogre, the way some of those girls dither around when I ask them to do anything!' He paused fractionally. 'However, I think I might have a solution. If you do my letters now you can come in early in the morning to finish the minutes. Surely that Howard woman can take the child to school for once? I'll pick you up at about eight.'

Hannah gasped. 'You really do think you can walk all over people, don't you? We don't all live and breathe work the same as you do. We do have a home life, which is pretty sacrosanct as far as I'm concerned. I don't see why I should shunt my son on to someone else simply to please you. The hours we spend together are precious.' She realised that she should not be talking to her employer in this manner, but he really did annoy her when he spoke about Daniel so carelessly.

'You'll be earning yourself extra money.'

'And you think that will solve everything—money?' she scorned. 'You think it's the answer to all problems?' Her face was a fiery red, caution thrown to the winds.

'As far as I can see,' he said, his tone calm, but all the more dangerous because of it, 'you're in dire need of every penny you can earn. A flat is no place to bring up a child. He needs a garden to play in, he needs space. You need a house.'

'You think I'm not aware of that, Mr Quest? It's on my mind constantly. But being with my son is more important to me than earning money. I realise you don't understand, having no family of your own, but that's the way it is. And you did know these things before you took me on as your secretary.'

'Yes, yes, I knew, I knew,' he exclaimed tetchily, 'but I didn't realise what a difference that hour would make.'

'I think that even if I worked normal hours you'd still find something you wanted doing at the last minute,' Hannah snapped back. 'You're a workaholic and expect the same of everyone else.'

'If you want to get on in this life you don't have to be afraid of hard work,' Jordan informed her tersely.

'You mean making money is the most important thing in your life?'

Suddenly he smiled. 'I think *you* could become important to me.'

Hannah gasped, 'Me?' This was the last thing she had expected. 'Why me?' Unless it was the female sex in general he was talking about. She could still picture the way he had spoken to Riva March a few minutes ago, his voice deep and intimate as though she meant more to him than any other person. It was clear he was like this with every girl he met.

'As I said the other day, you're both sensuous and beautiful, and you deserve a lot more out of life than you're getting at the moment.'

Meaning she needed a man to take her to bed! Hannah stared at him scornfully. 'I don't think my personal life is any of your business,' she said coldly.

'How old are you, Hannah? You really don't look old enough to be saddled with the responsibility of an eight-year-old child.'

He must know how old she was, he only had to look at her personnel records, but she jutted her chin and said firmly, 'I'm twenty-seven. I married when I was eighteen.'

'Had you known your husband long?' He leaned against the edge of her desk, seeming prepared to stay and talk for however long it took him to find out about her, his important work for the moment forgotten.

She sighed. 'Since I was fifteen. Why are you asking me all these things?'

'Because I'm interested in you. Was he your only boyfriend?'

Hannah nodded.

'And you want no one else? He must have been someone very special?'

'He was.'

'I'd like you to tell me about him.'

Hannah's patience deserted her. 'I'm sorry, I refuse to go into any more details about my private life. If you want your letters done before I go I'd better get on with them.'

'Forget the letters,' he crisped. 'I have no wish to appear rude or insensitive; all I'm trying to do is help. You're so detached, so withdrawn from everyday life.

You live in your own little shell, and it's not good for you.'

'I don't need help from anyone, especially you,' she said, looking at him coolly. She did not believe that his intentions were strictly honourable. He wanted more from her than she was prepared to give. Had the circumstances been different, had she never married, had there been no Riva March on the scene, then she might have fallen for his manifest charm. As things were, she wanted to keep as much distance between them as possible. And it was as well that he knew it.

'Do you intend to spend the rest of your life living on the memories of your dead husband?' he demanded.

Hannah gasped anew at his insensitivity, trying not to remember the fact that her parents had said exactly the same thing to her not so very long ago. She lifted her chin, her blue eyes defensive. 'Mr Quest, I think we should get one thing very straight. What I do, how I feel, is up to me. I don't want anyone else interfering. If you don't like the way I am, if you want more from me than I'm prepared to give, then I think we should call a halt to things right now. In fact, I think it's best. I resign.'

His face was a picture of astonishment and disbelief. Hannah almost wanted to laugh, but instead she walked round to her desk and sat down; if she hadn't her legs would have collapsed beneath her. She did not have to think about it to know that she had been very rude, that she had spoken completely out of turn. And to top it all she had thrown in the best job she'd ever had!

'Hannah.' Jordan followed her and now his voice was close in her ear. 'Hannah, don't be impulsive. You need this job as much as I need you to do it.'

She refused to look at him, instead she fiddled with a piece of paper on her desk. 'I'm not given to impulses. I had my doubts when I took the job, but the money was tempting and I thought it might work out. Now I can see that it won't. If I've caused you any inconvenience I'm sorry.'

'Hannah, I want you to stay.' His hands came down on her shoulders and she froze, her whole body stiffening and rejecting him. It was an entirely involuntary reaction, brought on by a desperate need to preserve the cocoon in which she had wrapped herself.

But although she felt him tense at her rejection he did not let her go. In fact the pressure of his fingers increased. 'You're doing yourself no good by acting like this. It's time you came out of mourning and entered the real world.'

'I am in the real world,' she insisted. 'You don't understand.'

'I understand you're afraid to let another man touch you. Relax, Hannah, I mean you no harm.'

She closed her eyes and drew in a deep breath, forcing her tense muscles to slacken.

'That's better. Now look at me.'

She did not want to look at him, she did not want to see those dark eyes that sometimes appeared as though they were looking right into her soul. He saw too much.

'Hannah.'

Still she fought her inner battle. But when his hand slid from her shoulder along the column of her neck, his fingers creeping beneath her hair, his thumb a gentle caress behind her ear, her eyes shot wide and she jerked away.

He smiled. 'So there is life inside you?'

'Of course. I never said there wasn't.'

'Will you stay and work for me?'

To say no would be to admit that he disturbed her—but wouldn't she be lining up more trouble for herself if she carried on? He was making his interest in her very clear.

'Think of your son, think what a difference the extra money will make to his life. Don't you owe him that much?'

Reluctantly Hannah nodded.

'Then you'll stay?'

'I suppose so.'

'Good. I knew you'd see sense.' His smile was warm and all-encompassing, as if she really meant something to him, as if there was no Riva March in his life. 'And you'll come in early in the morning to finish typing those minutes?'

To her intense surprise Hannah found herself agreeing. 'But it will be a one-off occasion.'

'Of course.'

He said it too easily and she knew that if something else cropped up that was equally urgent he would have no compunction about pressurising her again.

Hannah found it difficult to concentrate on his letters. She had always known he was a disturbing man, but the knowledge had now been pushed firmly home and it was going to be very difficult ignoring him. In fact she made so many mistakes that it was well after half-past four when she finally left, and she had to run all the way home so that she would not be late.

'You could have asked Jordan Quest for a lift,' said Yvonne with a grin. 'He's welcome here any time, you know that.'

It seemed every woman was interested in him except her, thought Hannah as she proceeded to tell Yvonne about his plans for the next morning. 'I hope you don't mind. I know it's an awful cheek, but he really does need those minutes. I wouldn't ask if it wasn't urgent.'

'Of course I don't mind,' said Yvonne at once. 'I'll take Danny to school every morning if you wish.'

But Hannah did not want to change her son's routine too drastically. She enjoyed taking him to school, seeing him mix with his friends; it was a part of his growing up that she did not want to miss.

'Will Mr Quest give me a ride in his car when he comes in the morning, Mummy?' asked Daniel when they were back in their own flat. 'Can he take me to school in it?'

Hannah grimaced. 'He won't have the time, darling.'

'I wish we had a car,' grumbled Daniel unhappily. 'All the children at school come in cars—and all the children at school have daddies. I want a new daddy. Why can't I have a new daddy? Why can't Mr Quest be my daddy, and then we'd have a better car than anyone else?'

'Danny!' Hannah was stunned by his question, even though it was put in all innocence. 'You shouldn't say things like that. Mr Quest is just someone I work for.'

'But I still want a new daddy. I want someone to take me to football matches and play games with me and——'

'Oh, Danny, I know you miss your father. I miss him too.' She pulled him into her arms and held him close, feeling tears prick the backs of her eyelids. It was the first time in ages that Danny had mentioned his father, and the first time ever that he had said he would like another one. But why had he picked on Jordan Quest, of all people?

After Daniel had gone to bed that night Hannah could not help thinking about what he had said. Was she truly being fair on him, shutting men out of her life for ever?

Was she being totally selfish? She hoped not. She was firm in her resolve that she wanted no one to take Roger's place. Daniel had never said anything like this before. Perhaps it was a one-off thing; perhaps he wouldn't mention it again?

Jordan Quest arrived early the next morning, well before eight, and Hannah had no recourse but to invite him into their flat when he came pounding at the door. Although she kept it clean and neat the furniture was cheap and the curtains thin, some of the carpets were threadbare, and she felt ashamed of it. But worse than that, she had been so busy getting Daniel ready, making sure he ate all his breakfast and had his school books in his bag, that she wasn't dressed herself. Beneath her well-worn blue dressing-gown she still wore her cotton nightdress, and her cheeks coloured in embarrassment.

'I'm sorry,' she said, 'I didn't expect you this early. Please sit down, I won't be long.'

His eyes missed nothing, the threadbare dressing-gown or the fact that she was almost naked beneath. It was a long slow appraisal that brought warmth to her skin and the blood surging through her veins. 'Take your time, I'm sure your son will keep me entertained. Isn't that right, Daniel?'

Daniel was not quite sure what it was Jordan Quest was asking him, but he nodded all the same. Hannah was just closing her bedroom door when she heard him say, 'When are you going to take me for a ride in your car, Mr Quest?' She turned back in horror, a reprimand ready on her lips, but Jordan was already answering.

'How about tonight when I finish work—that's if your mother approves?'

'She will, she will,' answered Daniel excitedly. 'Wow! Wait till I tell my friends at school!'

Hannah did not listen to any more. It seemed to her that this man was becoming a part of her life whether she liked it or not. And in his car on the way to the office he intruded even further. 'Now I've seen how small your flat is I'm even more convinced that it's not the right sort of environment to bring up a child,' he told her.

'I entirely agree,' she retorted tightly. 'You don't have to tell me. But it's no business of yours.'

'I don't like to think of you not getting the best out of life.'

Hannah shot him a flash of scorn. 'Do you show as much curiosity about the private lives of all your employees?' she queried.

'Of course not.'

'Then why single me out?'

'I've told you before, you interest me.'

'So much so that you spend time thinking about me—and the way I live? I think that's a bit out of order, Mr Quest!'

'When are you going to start calling me Jordan?'

'Never,' she replied coolly. Except in her thoughts. He was Jordan then, and her thoughts were far too scaring and intimate to ever admit—and getting more and more so!

'That's a pity, because it's difficult to strike up any kind of a relationship when you insist on being so formal,' he told her.

She threw another disdainful look in his direction. 'As I've told you before, I have no inclination to involve a man in my life.'

His jaw firmed. 'How does your son feel about that? Are you being strictly fair on him?'

'I don't have to answer that question.' Hannah shrugged.

'You mean you're evading it?' His brown eyes flashed in her direction and in that fleeting moment saw every expression on her face.

Until last night Hannah would have told him that her son enjoyed their life the way it was, but now her cheeks became tinged with colour as she remembered Daniel asking whether this man could be his new father.

'Is there something you're not telling me?' Her embarrassment did not escape him.

'Of course not. Please, I don't want to talk about my son.' She had never been more aware of Jordan. There was so little space in the car that it was impossible not to feel his aura of power and strength, to inhale his own particular brand of masculinity, to feel a need to open the door and fling herself out. She did not want any of these feelings, she did not want this awareness, she wanted to keep a distance between them. Yet it was becoming increasingly impossible!

When they found the road blocked by an accident Jordan did a swift and unexpected U-turn, glancing at her with a pleased grin as he did so, then frowning when he saw her pale face. 'Did I scare you?' he asked.

Hannah shook her head. 'No, it was the accident. I feel sick inside every time I see one.'

'Of course—your husband! I never thought,' he said quickly.

'I actually saw his accident,' she admitted, a shudder of horror riding down her spine at the memory. 'He wasn't in our car at the time, he was on business for the farmer, that's why I didn't know it was him. Apparently the brakes failed on the other car and Roger never stood a chance.' There was a quiver in her voice as she spoke, and her eyes smarted with unshed tears.

Jordan's hand reached out and touched hers. 'That's tough,' he said gently.

Hannah jerked away, not needing his sympathy, not wanting any physical contact at all. 'It's a long time, I should be over it, but I don't think I ever will be.'

'Not if you don't let yourself,' he offered softly. 'Or let someone else help you. I'd like to help, Hannah, I really would. Won't you let me into your life?'

CHAPTER THREE

JORDAN was already intruding into her private life far more than Hannah wanted or expected, and the strange thing was that she had no idea how it had happened. He was insidiously getting closer to her, and it was up to her to put a stop to it before things got out of hand.

'Haven't you forgotten Riva?' she asked bluntly, wishing they would hurry up and reach the office and thus put an end to this uncomfortable conversation.

'Riva doesn't mean a thing to me.'

Hannah threw him a swift disbelieving glance. 'That isn't what she told me in the office the other day.'

'Oh? And what did she tell you?' He looked amused that the blonde had been discussing him, but Hannah did not find it the least bit funny.

'She warned me off you, as a matter of fact.'

'And is that what all this hands-off stuff is about?'

'Goodness me, no,' she scorned. 'Her warning was a waste of breath. She's welcome to you.'

Her answer did not please him. His hands gripped the wheel until his knuckles grew white. 'Has it ever occurred to you that I may not want Riva to be a permanent part of my life?'

'What are you saying?' she taunted. 'That she'll do until someone better comes along? Am I the next one in line for the specialist treatment, except that things are not going according to plan because I refuse to succumb?'

Jordan gave a snort of anger, but his response was cut off when he was forced to brake heavily as a dog ran out into the road in front of them.

Hannah took the opportunity to add, 'Do you want to know what else Riva said?' She was far too wound up to exercise caution. 'She said that you've taken every single one of your previous secretaries to bed. So you see, I know exactly why you're chasing me. But it will never work. I would never be disloyal to my husband.'

By this time they had reached the office gates, and the second he stopped the car she jumped out. But it was futile thinking she could run away from him, because the main doors were locked and she had to wait for him to catch up with her and open them.

'You should never listen to gossip, Hannah,' he said as they walked sharply along the corridors side by side. 'People make it up to suit their own ends.'

'People like Riva, you mean?'

'If you like.'

'Why do you encourage her if your intentions aren't honourable?' she wanted to know.

His lips quirked. 'It depends what you mean by honourable. I'm not intending to marry her, if that's what you're thinking, and she knows it, but she's an amusing young thing and very good company.'

And probably very good in bed, decided Hannah bitterly. She couldn't imagine Jordan remaining celibate for any length of time. 'Do you plan never to get married?' she asked with great daring. She had always thought it odd that he was still a bachelor.

His mouth twisted derisively. 'People usually get married for love, but as I don't happen to believe in it then I'd say it's very doubtful. Unless the girl were willing to settle for something less.'

It was at least an honest answer, if not one Hannah had been expecting. 'I shouldn't think you'd have much chance of that, Mr Quest. I'd never marry a man I didn't love, nor would any other girl I know.' Although she supposed there were girls around who would marry a man for the state of his bank balance. And Jordan Quest was certainly no pauper.

'It all depends on the interpretation of the word love, don't you think? It's a word that's used loosely in a lot of directions. I don't think it has one single connotation.'

He sounded cynical, and Hannah wondered if he had suffered a bad experience in the past that made him like this. But she did not dare ask any further questions.

The day sped, but as Jordan was locked up in a meeting for most of the time she saw nothing more of him, for which she was thankful, and she hoped against hope that he would forget he had promised to take Daniel out in his car this evening.

But her prayers were not answered. He turned up at ten to six, and Daniel dived across the room to answer his knock, his face red with excitement. 'It's Mr Quest, it's Mr Quest!'

Hannah turned down Jordan's offer to accompany them; it would be nice to have a few minutes to herself. But if she had hoped to think of other things while he was away she was mistaken. He seemed to have taken over her mind. If she closed her eyes she could see a picture of his strong-boned face on the backs of her eyelids, if she looked around the room she could picture him sitting in the armchair where he had waited for her this morning. It was impossible to dismiss him. And all too soon they were back.

Daniel came running to her. 'Oh, Mummy, it was super! We went fast—you should have been with us!'

He swung back to Jordan, who had followed him into the room. 'Can I have another ride some time, Mr Quest?'

'Danny!' exclaimed Hannah at once, 'that's very rude!'

'Your son's excited,' said Jordan, 'don't scold him,' and to Daniel himself, 'I'll see if I can find the time.'

Hannah knew that none of this was for her son's sake; it was simply another way of getting through to her. He was using Daniel. Though why he was being so persistent when she kept telling him she wasn't interested she did not know. Unless it was for that very reason? Perhaps he saw her as a challenge? Perhaps no other girls turned him down? Perhaps his ego was dented?

'Can Mr Quest stay for tea?' asked Daniel eagerly. He had been far too excited to eat earlier. 'We're having boiled egg and soldiers.'

'My favourite.' Jordan's face was serious. 'But it's really up to your mother.' He switched his attention to Hannah. 'Would it be a great inconvenience?'

Not inconvenient—but very disturbing. No other man had joined them for a meal since Roger died, and although she knew she was being unreasonable she did not want him there. But how to say it without appearing rude? She really had no choice but to agree. She nodded. 'You can stay.'

Daniel whooped with joy, and Jordan gave a pleased smile. 'Thank you,' he said.

'Come and have a look at my train-set,' said Daniel, adding, with one eye on his mother, 'if you'd like to.'

'I'd be delighted,' agreed Jordan. 'Lead the way, young man.'

Hannah let out a deep breath when they left the room and stood for a moment with her hands on the table to steady herself. Their flat consisted of two bedrooms, a kitchenette, and a living room. They ate in the living-room and she had laid the table ready for their light tea. The room also held a small cottage suite which she had recovered herself in flowered chintz, a small bookcase, and a TV set in the corner. The brown carpet had been in the flat when they'd rented it, as were the faded yellow curtains.

She looked around it for a minute, trying to see it with Jordan's eyes. It must seem very poverty-stricken. Not for the first time she wished that she and Roger had not been so lax about taking out life insurance. She had never thought she would find herself in such a position. And Roger had never cared about material possessions, so their few sticks of furniture were second-hand and none of it worth very much.

The pan of water was boiling, and she put in three eggs, spreading some bread with margarine but not cutting Jordan's into fingers as she did for Daniel. She had some fruit cake that she had baked at the weekend, and she put that on the table as well.

Once the eggs were boiled she spooned them out and sat them in eggcups—with pictures of Garfield painted on them! Then she pushed open the door of Daniel's room to tell them that tea was ready. The sight that met her eyes made her turn away in tears.

Jordan had stripped off his coat and was sitting cross-legged on the floor. Opposite him sat Daniel in a similar position. Between them ran the trains that Roger had set up for his son at a very early age. Jordan had a whistle in his mouth and was obviously acting the part of the guard, Daniel was in charge of the controls. It was a scene Hannah had seen so many times before.

There was really no comparison between Roger and Jordan. Roger had been much shorter, with fair hair and a fresh, ruddy complexion due to working all his life out of doors. He had been powerfully built, but he certainly hadn't Jordan's excellent physique. Nevertheless, seeing him sitting there like that brought memories flooding back.

'Is tea ready?' asked Daniel.

She swallowed hard and nodded, and by the time they were seated at the table she had regained her composure.

'Mr Quest's brilliant. He knew the names of all my engines without me telling him,' announced Daniel.

'That's nice,' she smiled.

'Daniel tells me he's had no one to play with his train-set since his father died,' said Jordan.

'That's right,' answered Hannah sharply. 'Most of the little boys around here are too rough. I don't want it to get broken. My husband built the layout for Daniel. I sometimes play with him myself.'

'But not often, Mummy,' accused Daniel. 'You always say you're too busy.'

'Eat your tea, Daniel,' said Hannah, and the tone of her voice warned him that he was going too far.

It felt strange, Jordan eating with them, and she noticed that he cut his bread and butter into fingers, dipping them into the yolk of his egg in exactly the same fashion as her son. He would make a good father, she thought; it was a great pity he had no intention of getting married.

He ate with relish, his eyes on her frequently, sending a flurry of warm feelings through her, making her feel uncomfortable in his presence. He took a slice of cake when it was offered, complimenting her on her cooking. 'You must give my housekeeper the recipe; this is excellent.'

'I'm quite sure she can bake better cakes than me,' said Hannah.

'Nothing like this,' he assured her.

'Can Mr Quest come to my birthday party?' asked Daniel, feeling that he had kept quiet long enough.

Hannah gave him a look enough to kill. 'I don't think little boys' birthday parties are quite the sort of thing Mr Quest would like.'

'On the contrary,' said Jordan at once, 'I haven't been to a birthday party in years. It should be fun. When is your birthday, Daniel?'

'On Saturday, and I shall be nine,' he answered importantly.

'And are you holding your party here?'

'Yes,' said Daniel. 'We're having hot dogs and beef-burgers. Do you like them?'

'I love them, but I have a better idea—providing your mother approves, of course. How about having your party at my house? We could have it out in the garden if it doesn't rain, and you can still have your hot dogs. I have a swimming pool as well, if it's really hot. What do you say to that?'

Daniel clapped his hands and looked at his mother pleadingly. 'Can I, Mummy? Can I? It would be the best party I've ever had. Oh, please say yes!'

It would have been cruel to deny him such pleasure, so she nodded, even though she felt even more sure now that Jordan was using her son to get through to her. Why else would he take so much interest in the boy?

When they had finished eating Hannah sent Daniel to his room, and once they were alone she turned on Jordan. 'You had no right interfering in Daniel's party arrangements!'

'I felt sorry for the boy. It can't be any fun stuck in this flat all the time. You've made it very comfortable, but even so——'

'It is our home,' she told him coldly. 'By inviting Daniel to your house, which I've no doubt is very large and very opulent, you're going to make him unhappy here. He'll want better things, and I can't afford to give them to him.'

'You think I have an ulterior motive?'

'That's right.'

'What sort of a motive?'

'For some reason I fail to understand I think I'm your target. Haven't I made it clear that I have no interest in you?'

His smile was warm and amused. 'Very clear. But the pursuit is part of the attraction.'

'And you intend to use my son to get through to me?'

'No, I wouldn't do that, it's hardly fair. But I did think a party in my garden would be an extra special treat for him. He's a good lad, Hannah, you've brought him up well. He knows his manners and never speaks out of turn.'

'But he needs a man in his life—that's what you're still trying to tell me?' she asked bitterly, 'Please go, Mr Quest. I thank you for your offer, and I won't disappoint Daniel now, but please don't put any other tempting offers in his way.'

She walked with him to the door, but before he opened it he turned and put his hands on her shoulders. 'You're a courageous woman, Hannah Carpenter, determined and independent, and very, very attractive.' Before she could anticipate his actions he lowered his head and dropped a light kiss on her mouth. 'Goodbye, and thank you for the tea. You'll never know how much of a treat it was for me.'

The second the door closed behind him Daniel came bouncing into the room. 'He kissed you, Mummy, I saw him! Does that mean he loves you? Does that mean you're going to marry him? Is he going to be my new daddy?'

'No, Danny, it does not, and you shouldn't have been watching,' snapped Hannah.

He looked hurt by her brusque tone. 'But when you and Daddy kissed you said it was because you loved each other.'

'Mr Quest's kiss was a friendly kiss, nothing more—a thank-you for the tea. Have you tidied your room? If so I'll read you a story.'

Not until Daniel was tucked up in bed and asleep did Hannah let herself think about Jordan's kiss. It had been brief, and yet it had shocked her to the core. She had expected to feel repulsed; instead it had awoken feelings she had thought long since dead, feelings she did not want to experience where this man or indeed any man was concerned. Why, oh, why wouldn't he leave her alone?

She was almost afraid to go into the office the next morning, but Jordan had another meeting to attend and she was spared the embarrassment of facing him. It was just after lunch when her outer door opened and a fresh-faced young man came waltzing in without so much as a knock. He was heading for Jordan's door when he stopped short and looked at her, a broad appreciative smile curving his lips. 'You're new!' he announced.

'And you're out of order if you think you can walk straight into Mr Quest's office without an appointment,' Hannah told him sternly. She wasn't going to disclose that Jordan wasn't in his office.

'Mmm, fierce as well as pretty. A lethal combination.'

He continued to study her, and Hannah lifted her chin in swift irritation. 'Would you mind telling me your name and what your business is with Mr Quest?'

He laughed and carried on with his assessment. 'Mr Quest. Personal business.'

She frowned. 'Yes, but what is *your* name?' Did he always play games like this?

'Mr Quest,' he repeated.

She frowned. 'Quest? Then you're——'

'That's right, I'm Jordan's brother. Drew's the name—the fun-loving member of the family. Irresponsible, according to Jordan, but I'd dispute that. Why should I devote my life to trying to make money when it's much more fun spending it?' He strode towards her desk and held out his hand.

Hannah frowned, then laughed as well. 'Hannah Carpenter. And I didn't know Jordan had a brother.'

'If he hasn't told you about me it means you have a strictly business relationship,' he deduced. 'Which is good, even if it's unusual where my dear brother's concerned, because I've decided I want to ask you out. You're extraordinarily attractive, has anyone ever told you that?'

Hannah shook her head, trying to hide her laughter. There was no doubt about it, both these Quest brothers were endowed with smooth tongues, and Drew had just confirmed Riva's statement. So much for Jordan's saying it was all hearsay!

Drew was definitely the younger of the two, though his shoulders were as broad as Jordan's. His hair was dark, straight and short, but he was not so tall, and it was not easy to guess they were brothers. Drew's eyes were an unusual shade of green, somewhere between emerald and topaz, and they roved over her body like a caress. 'So how about it—can I take you out for dinner tonight?' he asked.

She gasped at his audacity, but could not help liking him for it. 'Thanks for the offer, but no.'

'Is there some other man in your life?' He pretended to look disappointed.

'You could say that. His name's Daniel and he's eight years old.'

'Oh!' For a second he looked taken aback. 'Is there a Mr Carpenter on the scene?'

'Actually, no, I'm a widow,' Hannah told him.

He smiled with relief. 'Some other time, then, when you can fix a baby-sitter?'

Still Hannah shook her head. 'I don't think so.'

'That's a pity, you look a fun sort of girl who'd like a good time.'

'I do?' No one had ever said anything like that to her before, especially since Roger died. Admittedly in the past she'd had her crazy moments—what young girl hadn't?—but all that seemed so long ago. She'd grown up a lot in the last few years.

'You most certainly do. Have you ever been to a casino? You can have the wildest time there. You must let me take you.'

Hannah laughed. 'What an impossible suggestion! I haven't money to throw away.'

'You might win,' Drew pointed out.

'Do you ever win?'

'Well, not exactly,' he confessed. 'But it's great fun trying. And I'm sure I'd be lucky with you at my side.'

'And I think Hannah would be luckier still if you kept out of her life.'

They both turned at the sound of Jordan's stern voice. Neither had heard him come into the room. Drew lifted his shoulders and smiled easily. Hannah felt uncomfortable, and the relaxed atmosphere Drew had engendered disappeared.

'What are you doing here at this time of day?' Jordan asked his brother brusquely.

Drew shrugged and avoided his eyes. 'I came to see you.'

'Then you'd better come into my office and let my secretary get on with her work.'

Drew followed Jordan, turning at the door to wink at Hannah. He had such a boyish, happy face that she could not help grinning in return. What a difference there was between them!

Soon their voices were raised in argument, although she could not hear what they were saying, nor did she want to. If it was some family dispute then it was best she shut her ears and got on with her work.

Shortly afterwards Drew came out. He did no more than give her a quick smile and another wink, but she could see that he was upset, and she wondered what Jordan had said to him.

He was followed by Jordan, who came up to Hannah's desk and frowned ferociously. 'You'd be well advised to steer clear of my brother. All he's interested in is a good time; he has absolutely no sense of responsibility.'

'He seems nice enough,' she defended. 'A lot of fun.'

Jordan frowned. 'He's the type you like, is that it?' His tone was harsh, his eyes condemning.

'I wouldn't say that, not exactly, but——'

'But you feel more attracted to him than you do to me? I couldn't help noticing how relaxed you were with him.' His nostrils were dilated, his eyes dark and narrowed, as though the whole idea of her liking Drew was abhorrent.

'He seems a very easy person to get on with. But as for suggesting that I feel anything for him when we've only just met, that's absurd.'

His expression turned sceptical. 'I hope, for your sake, that you're speaking the truth. Bring your notebook in, will you, I want to dictate some letters.'

He was always confident about what he wanted to say, but today he raced through his dictation even more quickly than usual, and Hannah had great difficulty in keeping up with him. It was as though he wanted to get them out of the way as quickly as possible because he had other things on his mind. Was it something to do with Drew? she wondered.

When he had finished he leaned back in his chair and closed his eyes, his legs stretched out, taking deep regulating breaths. Hannah sat and watched him for a moment. He never usually showed physical or mental tiredness; he seemed to have an inexhaustible supply of energy. But when she got up to leave his eyes snapped open. 'Wait a moment, Hannah, I want to discuss your son's party.'

And so she sat, watching him, a rare occasion when he was not observing her. He had taken off the jacket to his grey suit and loosened the knot in his tie. His hair was ruffled and fell untidily over his forehead, and she had an insane urge to smooth it back. She had not realised exactly how muscular he was. His jacket had never disguised the breadth of him, but now for the first time she saw his powerfully muscled shoulders and forearms and felt a shiver of excitement. Black springy chest-hairs thrust against the white silk of his shirt, and she had another demented urge to feel them beneath her fingertips.

With a start she realised Jordan was watching her. 'What is it, a comparison of the two of us?' he sneered, pushing himself straight in his seat. 'I can assure you Drew's a non-starter where women are concerned. He'll splash out his money—oh, yes, he likes spending money—but it doesn't go far when you spend it the way he does. He's just told me that he's lost yet another job.'

Hannah frowned. 'Why's that?'

'Because he's careless in his work, because he's a bad timekeeper, because he's totally irresponsible. All he cares about is having a good time. He's never liked work; that's why I would never have him with me.'

'What does he do? Or should I say what did he do?' she asked.

Jordan snorted his derision. 'He likes to think of himself as an artist, although he had an excellent education and can apply himself to most things if he puts his mind to it. He's actually quite clever. His last job was with an advertising company.'

'And now they've sacked him?'

'That's right.'

'Why did he come to see you?' asked Hannah.

'For the same reason as he always does when he's down on his luck—he wants a loan. But I've helped him for the last time. He's on his own. If he doesn't work he gets no money. And that won't suit him, because it means he won't be able to impress the fairer sex. And that could include you, Hannah.'

'Me?' she frowned. 'What's your brother got to do with me? I only met him for a few seconds.'

'A few seconds was enough to make an impression as far as he was concerned,' Jordan returned grimly, and there was a new hardness to his tone, a warning almost. 'He's had plenty to say about you.'

'Such as what?' she demanded.

'He wanted to know how long you've been working for me, what sort of a relationship we have—if any—whether there's any chance for him, what days you have off, et cetera, et cetera. He seems to have fallen for you quite heavily, though I wouldn't feel flattered by it if I were you—Drew changes his girlfriends as often as his shirts.'

'I hope you told him that I'm not interested in a relationship with you, him, or anyone else, and that I'm perfectly happy as I am?' she returned quietly but firmly.

'Let's say I convinced him that he would be wrong to pursue you.' Jordan's eyes glittered with an anger she could not understand.

'You told him I belonged to you?' she asked incredulously.

'I hinted at it.'

'You have a nerve! It's untrue and you know it! You're the last man I want as a permanent part of my life.'

'Who's talking about permanency?'

Hannah tossed her head with a flush of indignation. 'So it's an affair you're after? It's no more than I suspected, but not what you're going to get. Really, Mr Quest, I don't see the point in this conversation.'

'You're right, let's forget it,' he said, much to her surprise. 'All I wanted to do was put you straight about my brother. Now, about young Daniel's party.' He went on to tell her that all the arrangements had been made, it was due to begin at three. A clown was booked to entertain them and, weather permitting, there would be swimming in the pool. Mrs Braden, his housekeeper, was cooking the hot dogs and beefburgers, as well as lots of other fancy food she thought the children might like.

'You've gone to a lot of trouble,' Hannah said, feeling both embarrassed and grateful. 'How can I thank you enough?'

'There is a way.' Jordan's eyes warmed with a smile as he spoke.

Hannah looked at him warily. 'And that is?' She ought to have known there'd be a condition, that he hadn't offered Danny this party entirely out of the kindness of his heart.

'You could let me take you out to dinner. From what I understand, you never go anywhere. You deserve to be wined and dined and treated like a lady—at least once in a while.'

Hannah shook her head. 'Danny gets upset if I leave him—he thinks something might happen to me, the same as it did his father. He's getting better, admittedly, but I still don't like to ask anyone else to look after him.'

'You're each totally dependent on the other?'

'I suppose you could say that,' she agreed.

'It's wrong, Hannah; you should get the boy used to being left. You can't go on like this for the rest of your life. I'm sure Yvonne Howard would be delighted to look after him—she seemed to me a very willing sort of person. I'll ask her myself if you're reluctant. I don't think she'll refuse.'

Of course Yvonne wouldn't, not if Jordan asked her. He only had to turn on his famous charm and no one refused him anything. And certainly Danny wouldn't mind if she was going out with Jordan. He was his favourite person at the moment.

'In fact,' he went on, 'tomorrow night after the party would be perfect. Shall we call it a date?'

'How about Riva?' Hannah asked sharply. 'Won't you be seeing her?'

'Nothing's arranged,' he told her easily, though his tone suggested that he did normally see Riva on a Saturday night. 'And it's you I'm asking.'

Hannah fought an inner battle with herself and lost. He was being so kind to Daniel, it would be wrong to refuse. 'I'll come,' she said, 'just this once.'

'Good. You won't regret it, I promise.' His eyes were steady on hers, and Hannah felt a stirring of her senses, but also warning bells rang in her head telling her not to get too involved. It would be easy to do so. His attraction combined with his persistence were a lethal combination.

CHAPTER FOUR

DANIEL was beside himself with excitement when Hannah told him about the clown, and unable to sleep when she put him to bed. She had to read to him for almost an hour before his lids finally drooped and he gave way to his very real tiredness.

Hannah's biggest dilemma was what to wear when she went out with Jordan. She certainly could not afford a new dress, but which of her old ones would look best? None of them was very sophisticated. With Roger working late hours on the farm they had rarely gone out, and besides, money had been too short for fancy clothes. In fact she had bought very little for herself since Daniel was born. She'd virtually lived in jeans, T-shirts and sweaters. After Roger's accident when she had been forced to go out to work she had bought a few serviceable clothes, but certainly nothing that could be deemed suitable for an evening out with Jordan.

Her problem was solved when she thought of her friend Maggie. They had been at secretarial school together before either of them were married and still kept in touch. Maggie had married a bank manager and led a life far removed from Hannah's. Since Roger's death Maggie had done her best to fix Hannah up with someone else—all to no avail.

Now Hannah phoned her and explained her dilemma. 'My dear Hannah,' said Maggie at once, 'come over in the morning and take your pick. Who is this man? And am I glad to hear you're ready to start dating again! You've been a hermit for far too long.'

Danny was awake at six. Normally he sat in bed reading or writing until Hannah's alarm went off, but today he came into her room and touched her gently until she stirred.

'Happy birthday, darling,' she smiled, hugging and kissing him and struggling to sit up. 'Your present's on the chair.'

He had already spotted the parcel, and now he happily fetched it, sitting on the bed with her, tugging impatiently at the string. Inside were two other parcels, in the smallest a wristwatch. His face beamed when he saw it and he could not wait to put it on. In the second parcel was another railway engine to add to his collection. 'Wow! Wait till I tell Mr Quest!' he beamed. 'I bet he doesn't know what this one's called. I'm going to take it with me to show him.'

Three o'clock could not come soon enough for Daniel. He accompanied her reluctantly to Maggie's, kicking his heels impatiently while they caught up on the latest gossip and Hannah decided which dress to borrow. They did their normal weekly shopping and she bought him a new purple shirt to go with his best pair of trousers. Even so he was ready and dressed by one.

She was thankful the weather had remained fine so they would not get wet on their walk to the house. Jordan lived on Hunter's Hill, an exclusive residential area of this Staffordshire town where only the most affluent people lived, most of them millionaires. Hannah was taken completely by surprise when a car turned up at the door to fetch them. Even Daniel was stunned into silence at the sight of the uniformed chauffeur.

The car was a spacious maroon Mercedes 280 with the rich smell of new leather inside. Daniel scrambled in and whispered to his mother, 'Is this Mr Quest's as well? Why has he got two cars?' All the way to the house his tone was kept reverently low.

The whole afternoon was a little boy's dream. It could not have been more perfect. They were entertained, they swam, they played, they ate, Jordan joining in everything. He gave Daniel two tickets for Twycross Zoo as his birthday present, and he was ecstatic. Hannah was happy about it as well. She had been so afraid he might buy the boy something terribly expensive, something she could not possibly hope to compete with.

At the end of the day Daniel went to bed a happy and tired little boy, not at all disturbed that he was going to be left in the care of Mrs Howard because his mother was going out with Jordan Quest. In fact he was more than pleased about it. Hannah wished she felt the same. Now the time was drawing near she grew more and more nervous, and wished she had never agreed.

The dress she had borrowed was in lemon silk, the neckline scooped low, the skirt swirling in a myriad tiny pleats. With a white sash tied at the waist and white strappy sandals on her feet, her face made up and her hair arranged in a frame of soft curls, she looked beautiful and elegant—nothing at all like Daniel's mother!

It was like going out on a first date all over again, not knowing what to expect, afraid, shy, her heart practising hammer-beats within her breast, every one of her pulses racing.

Jordan arrived promptly, looking stunned when she opened the door. 'Reality is better than the dream,' he said softly. 'I've always thought you were beautiful, but tonight you're ravishing. You should dress up more often.'

Hannah did not state the obvious—that there was no point in dressing up when she had nowhere to go; she merely smiled and thought he looked pretty devastating himself. She was used to seeing him in dark business suits, but tonight, although he still wore a suit, he looked very different. It was so pale as to be almost white, a rich ivory, probably hand-made, and she guessed it had cost the equivalent of about six months of her salary. The silk shirt he wore to go with it was in ivory also, and his tie held the merest hint of beige, as did his shoes. He was spectacularly elegant, and Hannah thanked her lucky stars that she hadn't worn one of her simple cotton dresses. She would have felt like a country bumpkin.

Even so she felt gauche. This was a totally new experience. Roger hadn't believed in wasting good money on fancy restaurants, as he called them, preferring good, home-grown, home-cooked food, in the comfort of his own home.

It was the Mercedes tonight but minus the chauffeur, and Hannah settled into the soft leather seat feeling strange and yet excited too. Nothing like this had ever happened to her before. She had been out with no other man except Roger and was not sure that she knew how to handle it.

'Happy?' Jordan smiled warmly as he checked her seatbelt, then fastened his own. He wore a different brand of aftershave this evening, something exotic and spicy which invaded her nostrils and somehow added an extra air of excitement to the occasion. Her own perfume was a simple floral one that Daniel always said smelled of fresh air and buttercups. She did not know that buttercups had any particular scent, but if anyone else wore the same perfume he always said, 'That's Mummy's perfume.'

'Yes,' she said faintly. She was happy, even if a little anxious. She did not know what to expect from the evening, or indeed what Jordan expected of her! Things were moving far too quickly for her peace of mind. 'Where are we going?' she asked. She hoped it wouldn't be somewhere too exclusive where she would be completely out of her depth.

'My favourite place.' His hand briefly touched hers, sending a rush of excitement through her veins. Her adrenalin was already running high this evening, and she hoped against hope that he wouldn't push for too much. She was still adamant in her own mind that she wanted no other man in her life. 'I hope you'll like it too,' he went on after a moment's pause, a moment when her heart thudded so loudly that she felt sure he must hear. 'It's a seventeenth-century country mansion that's been converted into a superb restaurant. The food is excellent.'

'Is it far?' They were mundane questions and not important, but she wanted to try and prevent any intimacy between them.

'About half an hour. How's Daniel? Has he gone to sleep yet after his exciting day?' He seemed to know her mind was troubled by the two of them being together.

'Oh, yes!' Hannah was on home ground now and her voice brightened. 'He was totally exhausted. He's had a wonderful time, as did all his friends. I can't thank you enough for the trouble you went to. It really wasn't necessary to provide——'

'I did what I did because I wanted to,' Jordan interrupted firmly. 'If you want to know the truth, I've had a wonderful day too. I'd like Daniel around more often.'

'I'm afraid that's not possible.' Her tone was suddenly sharp. 'I don't want him to get spoilt. He's not used to such luxury, and it could make him critical at home. Surely you can see that?'

'I suppose so. It seems a pity, though, when——'

'Let's drop the subject.' It was Hannah's turn to intervene. What she had thought was a safe topic was now a dangerous emotional issue. 'I'm here because it's what you want, and it would be rude to refuse after you've been so good to Daniel. But after tonight there'll be no more visits to your house, and I won't come out with you again. It will be back to business as usual—*Mr* Quest.'

His hands took a firmer grip on the wheel and out of the corner of her eye she saw a tenseness in his jaw. It was a second or two before he spoke, and in his tone was a hardness that had not been there before. 'That's a pity. I really did think I was going to be allowed to get to know you better.'

'I'm afraid there won't be any chance of that,' she answered primly.

It was clear she had angered him, and in one way Hannah felt sorry that she had spoilt what could have been an interesting and refreshingly different sort of evening, but she did not want Jordan getting any wrong impressions. It was best that he knew how she felt. There was silence between them and she thought he was not going to speak again. She was thinking of suggesting that he turn around and take her home, when he suddenly growled, 'We're almost there.'

He left the main road and drove through acres of lovely parkland where fallow deer grazed and the peace of the countryside surrounded them. It was wrong to be at odds with one another somewhere as beautiful as this, Hannah thought. She sorely missed the wide open spaces. There were times when she actually grew homesick for the farm, even though going back there would, she knew, evoke too many sad memories.

The dozen or more windows of the red brick building they were approaching reflected the sinking sun like dozens of golden eyes, and inside it was a collector's paradise with paintings and tapestries, porcelain and silver, all on public display.

Jordan led her into an oak-panelled room where they sat down on blue velvet chairs. He ordered her a dry sherry which she sipped while studying the menu. The place was every bit as expensive and luxurious as she had feared, the prices of some of the dishes more than she spent on food in a whole week. 'What are you having?' she asked Jordan at length, reluctant to order something that was going to cost so much. It seemed such a waste of money.

'I thought I might have the *escargots* to start with. Have you ever tried them?'

Hannah shook her head and pulled a face, the very thought abhorrent.

'What a shame to wrinkle up so charming a nose!' He smoothed it with the tip of a firm warm finger, sending a fresh torrent of sensations through each and every one of her nerves. His eyes had lost their hardness and were a warm, friendly brown, watching intently every expression on her face.

It was too intimate here, thought Hannah in panic. Though there were several other people in the room, each was absorbed in his or her companion, and they might as well have been alone.

'And how can you be sure you won't like them?' Both his expression and his tone of voice suggested that he wasn't altogether thinking about food, that he was far more interested in her. 'They're an acquired taste, perhaps, but truly succulent. Be daring and have a go. You can always leave them if they're really too horrible and I'll order you something else.'

'But that would be a waste!' she said in horror, using the opportunity to jerk away from him. She never threw anything away; she could not afford to.

'If you don't like them then *I'll* eat them, my prudent little friend,' he told her with a smile that grazed over her skin, raising it in tiny little goose-pimples. He wasn't missing a single opportunity to let her know how he felt, thought Hannah, and she wasn't sure that she could endure such treatment for the whole evening.

'All right, you've convinced me,' she said faintly.

'And how about the salmon steak in champagne sauce for our fish course? Followed by medallions of veal?' His tone was low and vibrant as though he were whispering words of love instead of discussing the menu.

'That's fine.' She was glad to let him take over. He was having such a profound effect on her that the whole evening was beginning to take on an unreal air.

As the waiter came to take their order Hannah glanced about her. The room was hung with Regency cut glass chandeliers, the curtains were in blue velvet to match the chairs and the atmosphere was one of quiet elegance.

All too soon Jordan's attention was turned to her again. 'Do you know, Hannah, I know nothing at all about you,' he remarked.

'That's because we don't have the kind of relationship that invites confidences,' she told him, more sharply than she intended, but alarmed by the feelings he managed to arouse. It wasn't as if he was a man she could trust. She knew only too well that he wasn't serious about her, that this seduction was yet another scene in his game of life.

'We could have—if you'd relax a little.'

'I can't,' she said, so softly that he had to lean closer to hear. 'I'm not ready.'

'Hannah.' He took her hands into his, squeezing tightly when she tried to pull away. 'You have to start some time. You can't go on as you are for ever. I know I've said it's not fair on Daniel, but you're doing yourself no favours either.'

Hannah lifted her slender shoulders. 'Perhaps not, but that's the way I want it.'

Jordan had earlier moved his chair so that he was sitting directly facing her, their knees almost touching. 'I think,' he said, his tone low and deep and meaningful, his fingers playing with hers, 'that you're frightening other men off with that icy shell you've built around yourself. But——'

'I have not——'

'But I'm not other men, Hannah,' he went on, ignoring her interruption. 'I can be very persistent, and I will be. I want you to trust me, to confide in me. I want us to be friends.'

What sort of friends? she wondered bitterly. 'Lovers' would probably have been a better choice of word. Jordan wasn't the type of man to endure a platonic relationship. 'Mr Quest, please, I——'

'Jordan,' he insisted. 'It's time you called me Jordan.'

There was a hypnotic quality to his rich brown eyes and she found it impossible to look away. 'Jordan, then,' she said quietly. 'I can't do that, you're asking too much, too soon.'

She recognised the muscle that tensed in his jaw; it was becoming all too familiar when he did not get his own way. Nevertheless a smile lifted the corners of his generously sculpted mouth. 'But you're not rejecting me outright?' he asked.

She chewed reflectively on her lower lip. 'I suppose that's what I'm saying. You've got closer to me than any other man, I will admit that.'

'Perhaps it's not so much that you're not ready, it's that you're afraid?' An eyebrow rose in a question. 'If you've never been out with any other man except your husband then I can understand your hesitation.'

'You make me sound naïve!' she protested.

'That wasn't my intention, Hannah, but isn't it the reason you feel uneasy with other men? Not simply the fact that you believe you're not ready?'

Hannah debated his question, wishing he would let go her hands. How could she answer honestly while feeling the full impact of his sexuality? He was so different from Roger, so much more a man of the world. Theirs had been a simple life. She had never been questioned before about her feelings; there had been no need. She had not even thought very deeply about them herself. And now she did not know how to answer. In the end she said truthfully, 'I think the reason I feel uncomfortable with you is that you're my employer.'

Jordan gave a snort of annoyance, his patience beginning to wear thin. 'That's an excuse and you know it! And even if you do feel like that at the office, it should make no difference now. Trust me, Hannah. Relax. For once you don't have to worry about Daniel—he's happy, and he's in good hands. Enjoy yourself.'

At that moment, much to Hannah's relief, they were told that their table was ready. The restaurant was large but tasteful with pink tablecloths and candles, exquisite crystal glasses and gleaming silver cutlery. They were

shown to a table in a corner alcove which set it apart
from the rest of the room. Intimate was the word that
sprang to Hannah's mind, and she wondered whether
Jordan had asked for this table specifically when he made
their reservation.

Once she was seated, the napkin draped on her lap by
an attentive waiter, the *escargots* were placed in front of
her. Much to her surprise Hannah found that she liked
them.

'You see,' said Jordan, suppressing a grin, 'you can
never be sure about anything until you try it. It's fun to
experiment.'

If you could afford to, thought Hannah drily. People
with money rarely gave a thought to the fact that some
individuals had to count every penny they spent.

'The same as you'll never know what it's like to be
more than an employee to me, unless you try it,' he
added. There was a meaningful gleam in his eyes, but
before she could retaliate he changed the subject. 'Tell
me something about yourself—I really know surprisingly little. Have you any brothers or sisters?'

She shook her head. 'I'm an only child.'

'How about your parents, where do they live? I never
hear you mention them.'

'In Scotland. They moved up there to look after my
grandfather. He's dead now, but they liked it so much
they stayed. I don't see them very often. I take Daniel
in his summer holidays, but that's all. How about you,
what sort of a family have you got?' Hannah did not
like all this interest he was showing in her.

'There's just Drew and me, and our parents, of course.
They live in Derbyshire now, in a picturesque little
cottage in Doveridge. I'll take you and Daniel there some
time. I'm sure you'll love it—it's right in the heart of

the countryside. My father potters about in his garden and my mother does work for charity. They're very happy there. They used to live at Hunter's Hill, but when my father retired and handed the business over to me I got the house as well.'

'How about Drew, does he live on his own or with you?' she asked.

'Unfortunately, he lives with me.' Jordan's brow darkened as he spoke. 'We're joint owners, but he never coughs up when it comes to paying the bills. He always swears he hasn't two halfpennies to rub together, though he enjoys tearing around in his Lotus Esprit. It was my parents' unfortunate gift to him on his twenty-first birthday. He treats the house more like a hotel than a home. Mrs Braden is forever tidying up after him. The one good thing is that he can't use his half of the house to borrow money against without my consent. My father was very wise in that direction, thank goodness.'

'Has he always been a spendthrift?'

'Always, right from when he was a boy. His pocket money never lasted him two minutes, and my parents indulged him and handed out more when it was gone. He almost died when he was born, you see, and my parents regarded it as a bonus when he lived. Consequently he was always spoilt. But why are we discussing Drew when you're a much more interesting person?'

His eyes were warm on her face, and Hannah felt a glow creeping through her that she was not sure she wanted. In her own way she was happy—happy with her memories—and Daniel. Letting Jordan become a part of her life could lead to all sorts of complications.

Their fish course appeared, their wine glasses were filled, and Hannah tried to concentrate her whole attention on the food. But it was difficult when she knew

Jordan was watching her, and against her will her eyes were drawn to his time and time again.

The warmth in her became a fire, and she knew that before the end of the evening she would find herself in his arms. With the strongest will in the world she would not be able to resist.

'Are you happy?' His tone was a husky growl, his smile all-encompassing.

Hannah wriggled on her seat and tried to stop herself meeting the intoxicating influence of his eyes. But it was impossible; it was as though her own eyes were drawn to his by a magnet and she saw much more than warmth, she saw raw desire, and it gave her quite a turn to see his feelings so openly displayed. She swallowed hard, nodded, then dragged her gaze away. 'This is a really lovely place. Do you eat here often?' She did not realise how breathless she sounded.

'Only when I want to impress someone,' he answered softly and meaningfully.

Hannah delved back in her memory and recalled making a booking for him here on more than one occasion. What she couldn't remember was whether they were business dinners, or whether he had asked her to book a table for two only, not saying who his companion would be, and she had assumed it was a girl he was taking out. There had been many girls; she had ordered flowers and taken phone calls often enough. But the thought that he might have brought any of them here, especially Riva, made her feel sick with jealousy—which was ridiculous when she felt nothing for him, when she hadn't wanted to come out with him in the first place.

'Is something wrong?' Jordan saw the fleeting expression of anguish.

She conjured up a smile. 'Of course not.'

'What were you thinking to bring such a shadow to your face?'

She lifted her shoulders in a graceful little gesture. 'Nothing, really.'

'Were you perhaps wondering whether I'd brought any other girls here?'

His astuteness astounded her. 'The thought did cross my mind,' she confessed.

'And it bothered you?'

Hannah was always totally honest, but on this occasion she felt justified in prevarication. 'Why should it? Of course you must have brought other girls here, it's that sort of place.'

'As a matter of fact, Hannah,' a slow, pleased smile crossed his face, 'I haven't. It's really rather special, don't you think? Where one would bring only a very special person.'

Her eyes widened.

'You didn't think you were special?' he added.

'Not really. How can I possibly be when you've never taken me out before? When you know so very little about me?'

'Oh, believe me, Hannah, you're a very special lady. All I have to do is convince you that you feel the same about me.'

She closed her eyes briefly. She did not want this sort of talk from Jordan, it was more than she could handle. 'There's only one special person in my life,' she said firmly, 'and that's Daniel. There's no room for anyone else.'

CHAPTER FIVE

JORDAN'S face stiffened, his eyes losing the warmth of desire, impatience taking its place. 'That's foolish talk,' he rasped. 'You can't cut out the rest of the world just because you've lost the man you loved. Do you think Roger would want you to remain single for the rest of your life? Is that what he wanted? Did you discuss it?'

'Of course not,' said Hannah quickly.

'If he loved you as much as you appear to have loved him then I'm sure he'd want you to be happy.'

'I am happy.'

He snorted angrily. 'What sort of happiness, when you have no other company than that of a child? And how about when he's older and out most of the time? What then? The longer you leave it, the older *you* get, the less chance you'll have of forming relationships.'

'I hadn't thought that far,' admitted Hannah with reluctance. Why did he have to dig so deeply? Why couldn't he leave her alone?

'I guessed as much,' Jordan sighed. 'I suggest it's time you did give it some thought. I really can't see why a beautiful young lady like yourself should become a hermit.'

'I'm not a hermit,' she snapped in her own defence. 'I go out to work, I meet people then. I meet my neighbours, other mothers.'

'But no members of the opposite sex,' he pointed out.

'And that's the way I like it,' she said tightly. 'You have no right to try and interfere in my life!'

'I'm only saying what I think is good for you.'

'When I want your opinion I'll ask for it.' She put her knife and fork straight on the plate and sat back, her breathing deeper than it had been earlier, her whole body feeling out of sorts with itself. She was running the whole gamut of emotions this evening. Why, oh, why couldn't he leave her alone? Why did he always pressurise her? And why had she agreed to come? It had been a foolish lapse on her part, she should have known it wouldn't work out.

Their plates were taken away and she twirled the stem of her glass between her fingers, watching the pale clear liquid, wishing there was a way she could magic herself out of here.

'I had such high hopes for this evening,' Jordan said at length.

Hannah had never seen him look so frustrated, but it wasn't her fault. 'You thought you were going to get somewhere with me?' she asked scornfully. 'Well, I'm sorry if I've let you down, but that's the way things are. I thought you knew it, I thought I'd already made my feelings clear.'

'Tell me something, Hannah.' He leaned forward across the table. 'Is it me personally you object to, or men in general? I seem to remember you were getting on pretty well with my brother when he came into the office the other day.'

'I want no man,' she told him simply. 'It would be totally disloyal to Roger.'

'After two years?' His mouth set into a grim, impatient line, and at that moment the waiter appeared with their main course. But Hannah's appetite had gone and she pushed the food around her plate until in the end Jordan suggested they leave.

There was an atmosphere now between them. The intimacy Hannah had felt in the car earlier was gone, and he was reacting as though it were her fault! Yet all she had done was confirm that she wasn't ready to let any man into her life. For some unknown reason it had made him angry, and she did not see why. There might come a time when she did feel something for him, she could not deny that she felt a certain attraction, but not yet, and never if he continued to push her.

She had hoped, when they got home, that he would drop her off, but instead he walked with her to the door, taking the key from her and opening it, then holding her elbow firmly to accompany her inside without so much as a word.

Yvonne looked up in surprise, her eyes going swiftly from one to the other, frowning slightly when she saw their tense faces. 'I'll go,' she said at once. 'I haven't heard a peep out of Danny. I'll see you in the morning, Hannah. Goodnight, Jordan.' It was clear by her expression that she was dying to know what had gone wrong, why they were home so early.

'I'll just take a look at Danny,' Hannah said once the door was closed behind her neighbour. 'Then I'll make us some coffee.' The last thing she wanted was to entertain Jordan, but he seemed to be giving her no choice.

'Have you nothing stronger?' he growled, prowling around the room like a caged animal, his hands pushed deep into trouser pockets, a frown drawing black brows together.

'I'm afraid not.'

'Because you can't afford it?' he suggested brutally.

'Because I rarely drink myself,' she hissed.

'And of course you never entertain the male sex?'

Hannah glared savagely. 'If the only reason you've invited yourself in here is to insult me then I suggest you turn right around and go!'

'I'm here because I thought we needed to talk,' he told her.

Her brows rose in sudden surprise. 'Isn't that what we've been doing all evening? And look where it got us. I can't imagine what else there's left to talk about. Haven't I made it clear where you stand? No amount of persuasion will make me change my mind. Did you think I'd be an easy pushover, is that it? You thought if you wined and dined me in romantic surroundings the rest would automatically follow? I'm sorry if I've disappointed you.'

'*You're* sorry?' he rasped. 'You're not half as sorry as I am! Tonight is going nothing like I planned. What astounds me is that you're not even prepared to meet me halfway.' Catching her shoulders in a grip as firm as iron, he gave her a little shake. 'I know I'm not totally repulsive to you, I know you find me attractive, so for pity's sake, Hannah, why don't you relax and enjoy yourself for once?'

She eyed him stolidly. It totally amazed her that whatever she said made no difference. Perhaps she ought to try another tactic? 'Haven't you ever stopped to think that I might not want to compete with Riva March?' she queried.

He snorted his impatience. 'I've told you Riva means nothing to me.'

'But she's still a part of your life. Besides, I have no wish to be one of a long line of conquests.'

Jordan's eyes narrowed. 'So that's it? That's the real reason you want nothing to do with me? You don't approve of my lifestyle?'

'I couldn't care less what you do,' she flung back angrily, 'just so long as you don't involve me. Will you let go of me so that I can check on Danny?'

'If there were anything wrong he'd be calling out for you,' he answered coldly. 'I'll let you go when I'm good and ready. It's about time someone injected a bit of life into that cold-blooded body of yours.' In one swift, violent movement he pulled her forcefully against him.

'Jordan, no!' cried Hannah, while at the same time a fury of emotions erupted. Reject him she might have done, but she was not exactly immune to him. The hours they had spent together had lit sparks of awareness inside her, and now they were in danger of igniting into something much more powerful.

She closed her eyes, not wanting to look at him, not wanting to respond to his compelling masculinity, inhaling instead his pungent aftershave, then discovering it was doing just as much to her senses as was the feel of him.

It was futile trying to evade his descending mouth, and contact was like an electric shock. His lips tortured hers with bruising hardness, and her body trembled against his. There was no letting up, the harsh assault continued, and the torrent of feelings inside her raged until they threatened to overflow.

No man had touched her for two years, and Jordan had worried at her senses ever since she began to work for him. This moment had been inevitable.

'Hannah,' he groaned. 'Oh, Hannah, how I've waited for this!'

She felt her defences crumbling, her reserve breaking, her body melting against his. It had been so long since she had felt like this, so long. Her body was blossoming with feeling she had thought long since dead. It was becoming alive, and without conscious thought she pressed closer, revelling in the feel of his throbbing, hard body against hers.

He gave an almost imperceptible pause while he acknowledged her submission, and then his tongue parted her burning lips to explore in triumph the moist heat of her mouth.

Hannah urged herself against him, moving unconsciously, heedful only of a driving need, a compelling ache that was taking a stranglehold on her senses.

His hand slid the yellow dress from one shoulder to cup the soft roundness of her breast, creating a fresh torrent of sensation. A deep shudder raged through her, and she wanted to cry out in ecstasy, and her elation grew as he nuzzled the soft skin of her throat, his lips and tongue searing a path towards her throbbing breast.

Her nipple had peaked and hardened beneath the tortuous teasing of his fingers and the throb of her heartbeats echoed loudly inside her head. She was delirious with excitement and desire, her own hands feverishly moving across his muscled back, wanting to lift his shirt too and revel in the touch of naked skin beneath her fingertips. She wanted to—— Was she out of her mind? What was happening? This was wrong, all wrong. She did not want Jordan; she loved Roger still, she always would. She wanted no other man.

She tore herself away from him, her face aflame now with shame and humiliation. How could she have let Jordan kiss her? How could she have reacted so wantonly? Oh, God, what was happening to her?

He let her go instantly, but his eyes glittered with furious anger. 'What the hell's the matter now?' he demanded.

'I—I can't go on with this,' she stammered unhappily. 'I don't want you to touch me, not now, not ever.'

'My God, Hannah,' he rasped, 'you certainly choose your moments! What's wrong—are you afraid of your own feelings? Were you giving too much away? Answer me,' he snarled when she gazed at him in mute anguish. 'You had the opportunity to stop me; why didn't you take it? Why wait until we got this far?'

The stone-cold fury in his eyes was like a slap in the face, and Hannah fell back. Anger on this scale was the last thing she expected. She had thought he might be hurt because she had put a stop to the kiss, but nothing like this. He was glaring at her as though she had committed some heinous crime.

'*You* started it,' she claimed sharply. '*You* knew how I felt!' Her own temper was beginning to rise to match his.

His breath hissed out through his teeth. 'If anyone's to blame it's yourself. You're the first girl who's ever pushed me away from her. I've never let myself get into that sort of a situation. I've never kissed a girl until I judged she was ready. And you were ready, Hannah—you can't deny it.'

She closed her eyes and clenched her hands together to still their trembling. He spoke the truth, there was no doubt about it. And she had actually enjoyed the experience—until sanity asserted itself! Until she realised where this sort of behaviour could end.

'Hannah, you have to let go some time.' His tone was quiet now, he seemed to have himself under control, though she was not sure how long this tenuous hold on his temper would last. He seemed capable of flaring up at the slightest provocation.

'I will,' she agreed faintly, 'but not yet, it's too soon.'

Jordan gave an exclamation of annoyance. 'Too soon! *Too soon?* I'm fed up with hearing you say that. Too soon in our relationship? Or too soon after your husband's death?'

Hannah cringed at the cold brutality in his tone. How could he speak of Roger so unfeelingly? Didn't he know how much she loved him? She crossed her arms and rubbed her chilled limbs. 'Both,' she told him bitterly.

He shook his head as though unable to understand her. 'Hannah, it's not been two weeks, or two months even, but *two whole years*. If you don't let go now you never will. I know you'll never forget him. I know you'll always think of him with love and affection—that's natural—but it's unhealthy to let him rule your life for evermore. And as for saying it's too soon in our relationship, that's ridiculous. I've known you altogether for three months. How can that be too soon?'

Hannah clenched her teeth, her lips moving as a whole host of emotions and thoughts ran through her mind. 'I just know it is, that's all,' she said firmly.

'And how long do you think it will take before you're ready to let me kiss you?' he sneered, brown eyes glittering.

She swallowed with difficulty, wishing he wouldn't pressurise her like this. 'I can't say.'

'You can't say!' There was harsh contempt now in his tone. 'Perhaps you can tell me this, Hannah. What are your feelings towards me?'

She did not want to answer this question and looked away, looking anywhere but at him. She did not even know herself what her feelings were. Jordan was like no other man she had met—devastatingly attractive, but far too overbearing for her peace of mind. He threatened her sanity, she felt vulnerable whenever he was close. She wanted him and rejected him both at the same time.

'Well, is the answer so hard?' His voice was a harsh rasp in her ear and a hand came up to turn her face back to him, fingers biting painfully into her chin.

'I suppose I do like you,' she confessed at length.

'You *like* me!' he sneered contemptuously. 'What sort of an answer is that supposed to be? How much do you like me?'

Hannah wished he wouldn't put her through the third degree. This was neither the time nor the place. She wanted to check on Daniel; it was a wonder their raised voices hadn't woken him. What if he were lying awake listening? What if he were upset? 'I suppose quite a lot,' she conceded.

'And what sort of form does this liking of yours take?' he insisted. 'Do you like me as an employer? You find me fair and generous and understanding, is that it? Or as a friend, maybe? Willing to listen and advise and console. But not as a lover? You could never see me in that light? Is that it, Hannah?'

He was making it so difficult for her. She was not used to being faced with decisions like this. And did she really know the truth herself? He was the best boss she had ever had, that was true, and he could possibly be a good friend. But he seemed to want more from her than friendship, and could she give him that? Did she like him enough? Was he right—was it really time to push Roger to the back of her mind and begin her life again?

The fact that her heart had begun to play tricks on her when he was around, the fact that her pulses raced when he touched her, told her that she liked him more than on a simple platonic level, but she did not feel at this stage that she could tell him. She did not feel it would be right to let these new feelings take precedence over those she felt for Roger.

When she was so long in answering Jordan let her go in disgust. 'I think your silence is answer itself,' he said coldly.

'No!' Hannah was quick to correct him. 'I do feel something for you, but I'm not yet ready to—to——'

'Admit it,' he finished for her cynically. 'Were you as indecisive in your feelings for Roger? Did you keep him guessing while you made up your mind?'

'That's despicable!' Her tone was sharp, her blue eyes bright. 'Besides, our relationship was totally different.'

'You had no hang-ups then, is that what you're trying to tell me?'

'It's not exactly the way I'd put it myself, but I suppose it's true,' she admitted. 'You've met me at a bad patch in my life.'

'One you're determined to prolong indefinitely,' he snorted. 'I think it's time I went.' He strode across the room without even looking at her again.

Hannah hurried to catch him up. 'Thank you for taking me out, Jordan. I'm sorry it's ended like this.' She was suddenly anxious to put things right between them.

'Not half as sorry as I am,' he grunted. 'Goodnight, Hannah.'

The door snapped decisively shut before she could say anything else, and although a moment before she had been anxious to check on Daniel, now she stood and leaned against it and let her thoughts run riot. She felt different, there was no getting away from it, and it was Jordan's kiss that had changed her. A kiss is just a kiss, so the song went, but Jordan's kiss wasn't simply a kiss, it had woken feelings that had lain packed in ice, that she had never expected or even wanted to feel again, and although she knew the road to recovery was still long and difficult, a glimmer of light now lay at the end.

She moved eventually and checked on Daniel, relieved to see him sleeping peacefully, and then threw herself down on the bed without even taking off Maggie's dress. She felt totally exhausted, both mentally and physically. What a night it had been. What a day! So much had happened in such a short space of time.

Jordan was Daniel's hero, there was no doubt about that. Jordan had joined in every game, even in their antics in the pool. He had been one of them, a boy again, reliving his own childhood. But tonight he had been a different person, all male and very sensual, seducing her with body language, making her feel extremely feminine—more so, she hated to admit, than Roger ever had.

There was something different about Jordan. Roger had been an ordinary, down-to-earth man, with a no-nonsense approach to things. He had loved her, yes, but he had never got sentimental about it. Once they were married he had never told her again that he loved her. She was supposed to accept that he did and get on with her life. And indeed she had been happy enough.

Jordan, she suspected, would be the sort of man who always sent red roses on birthdays and anniversaries—even if he got his secretary to do it for him! He would never fail to compliment a girl on what she was wearing, he would ensure that she knew how he felt, and he would go out of his way to make her feel wanted and loved. And yet he had never married. He said he didn't believe in love. So what was it he wanted from her? Hannah already knew the answer. An affair! This was probably the subconscious reason why she had rejected him, even though every female instinct in her responded.

It was a long time before she summoned the energy to take off the dress and her make-up and brush her teeth, and sleep came surprisingly easily. She had thought she would lie awake a long time thinking over the events of the day, but the next thing she knew it was daylight and Daniel was urging her to wake up. 'Mummy, Mummy, I want to go to the zoo!'

Hannah groaned and cast a sleepy eye at the clock. It was only seven, and Sunday morning! 'Another day, Daniel. Go back to bed now, it's far too early to get up.'

Disappointment shadowed his eager face. 'I want to go now. Mr Quest said he'd come with us.'

'He did what?' She sat up in bed fully awake. 'When did he say that?'

'Yesterday. He promised.'

Jordan had said nothing to her about it, and after last night she doubted whether he would honour his word. But if she refused to go then Daniel would be doubly disappointed.

'All right, we'll go,' she said, 'but it's still far too early. Go and play with your toys and let Mummy lie in a bit longer.' She would have to check on the buses, and it would be quite a jaunt. She was not sure that she felt up to it. Last night had left her physically and emotionally drained. But she could not let Daniel down.

'When will Mr Quest be here?' His face was all smiles again.

'I don't know, darling, but if he's not here by ten we'll go on the bus.'

'I don't want to go on the bus, I want to go in Mr Quest's car,' he said petulantly.

'That's enough, Daniel!' Her tone was sharper than she intended, and Daniel went very quiet, the way he always did when he was upset. He rarely argued with her, he always accepted her ruling, but he withdrew inside himself and usually went away somewhere to sulk. He walked from her room now, and Hannah let him go. It was very unfortunate that Jordan had promised to go with him to the zoo. She wished he'd had a word with her first.

It was no good trying to go back to sleep, but she lay there for over an hour before she got up to make Daniel's breakfast. And before nine o'clock Jordan put in an appearance! Daniel, who had been looking out of the window, saw his car pull up and ran excitedly to the door. 'It's Mr Quest, Mummy—I knew he'd come, I knew he would!'

Hannah felt her stomach churn as the door opened and Jordan stepped inside. But he gave her no more than a brief, cool nod before smiling warmly at her son.

'Mummy said you wouldn't come,' said Daniel eagerly, 'but I knew you would, because you promised.'

'I never break a promise,' he told Daniel gravely. 'I hope you're ready?'

Daniel looked at him indignantly. 'Of course I am!'

'And you, Hannah?' Jordan looked at her properly for the first time. 'Are you ready?'

Her pulses reacted swiftly to his steady brown gaze, but she kept her tone cool. 'Are you sure you want to come with us?' she asked.

He scowled at her less than obvious welcome. 'I couldn't let the child down,' he muttered grimly. 'I know I'm not your ideal choice of companion, but I suggest that you make an effort and at least pretend to be enjoying yourself.'

There was an underlying electric current running between them, and Hannah was not sure whether it was hostility or a simmering sexual tension. The moment

Jordan had entered the room she had felt his presence more strongly than ever before, as though her feelings for him had changed overnight. Which was ridiculous. She knew without a doubt that he would never take Roger's place.

Twycross Zoo, in Leicestershire, was very busy on this fine summer day. It had taken about an hour to get there, and Hannah had been conscious of Jordan for every second of that time.

He wore pale blue trousers and a white open-necked shirt, and he filled the Ferrari sports car with his presence. He was not a man you could ignore at the best of times, but in a confined space like this Hannah felt every one of her senses respond. She chatted to Daniel in the back seat in an effort to take her attention from Jordan, but it was an impossible situation when he was sitting so close beside her, when his arm came dangerously near every time he changed gear, when his aftershave was as heady as champagne.

'Let's go and see the monkeys,' said Daniel at once, taking hold of Hannah's and Jordan's hands and eagerly dragging them along. The last time she had taken him to the zoo, when he was about five, the chimps had been having a tea-party, and he had never forgotten it.

But they discovered the party wasn't until later, so they wandered around looking at the other animals, Daniel reading the name-plates on the cages or enclosures, Jordan helping him with some of the more difficult ones.

They looked like a family, she thought, and Daniel seemed to be turning more and more to Jordan for advice, or to share a thought. It was surprising how well they got on together. Even Roger had never had this complete rapport. No, that was wrong, father and son had loved each other dearly, but Roger had worked long and hard hours and hadn't the time to spend with Daniel that he would have liked.

Daniel was quite grown-up for his age, and Jordan on the other hand had no difficulty at all in bringing himself down to her son's level. Not that he talked down to Daniel—he didn't, he treated him as an equal, as a serious little adult. Hannah felt strangely hurt and perhaps a little jealous that Daniel should transfer his affections so easily. She would have to make sure her son didn't see too much of Jordan in future. It wasn't good for him to become too attached to this man.

Finally it was time for the chimpanzees' tea party, and as Daniel watched them, enthralled, firmly positioned at the front of the crowd, Hannah and Jordan stood well back. 'Daniel's thoroughly enjoying himself,' he remarked.

Hannah smiled and nodded her agreement. 'He's having a wonderful time.'

'How about you?' His eyes sought hers. 'Are you having a wonderful time as well?'

Hannah would have been lying if she said no. She was actually enjoying today far more than she had thought possible, but she had no intention of letting Jordan know this. 'Yes, it's very nice.'

'Very nice!' he echoed, a sudden flare of anger in his eyes. 'What sort of a reply is that?'

'I am enjoying myself,' she insisted.

'Because of Daniel—or me?'

'You're surely not asking me to choose between the two of you?' she asked in disbelief. 'There's no choice where Danny's concerned, he's my whole life.'

'And you're not going to let anyone else take a part in it?' There was cruel hardness now in his tone, a whiteness to his lips.

'That's not fair!' she protested.

'It's the way I see it,' he snarled.

Hannah turned away and tried to peer through the crowd to find Daniel. Why did Jordan always make things so difficult for her? Why was he trying to force her into a relationship she was not ready for? When his fingers caught her chin in a bruising grip, turning her face back towards him, she cried out in protest. 'Jordan, that hurts!' Her jaw was already tender from where he had gripped her yesterday.

'I don't like being ignored.' His fingers relaxed and his touch became a caress. 'We have a few minutes to ourselves; let's make the most of them.' His head swooped, his lips fiercely claiming hers, and she knew that if she tried to move his hold on her would tighten mercilessly.

Hannah had never before been kissed in such a public place, and she felt extremely self-conscious, even though no one saw; they were all too engrossed in the antics of the chimps. She and Jordan could have been the only two people in the zoo.

When he spoke again his tone was low and urgent. 'Hannah, I refuse to accept that you want nothing to do with me. I think you're all confused in your mind and need someone like me to sort you out. From now on I'm not going to take no for an answer.'

CHAPTER SIX

HANNAH wished she could believe it was an idle threat, but Jordan was not the type to say something and not mean it. She tried in vain to pull away, but his powerful arms became her prison. Panic quickened her heart and accelerated her pulses—or was it the feel of him against her? The heat of his hard, disturbing body? Or even memories of last night's kiss which had been far too unsettling for her peace of mind? For whichever reason, she wanted to be free of him.

'Hannah, I'm not letting you go until I have your word that you're going to stop fighting me.' His voice was a low, sensual growl in her ear, although he could have shouted at the top of his voice and no one would have heard. Everyone was concentrating on the antics of the animals in the cage. 'You're driving me insane, don't you know that?'

She risked a glance into the soul-destroying heat of his eyes. 'I think you're exaggerating. We've hardly spent enough time together for you to feel that way about me.'

'I know how much I want you.'

'That's right,' she whispered brokenly, 'you *want* me. But that's all there is to it, and I refuse to be any man's plaything.'

'Hell, Hannah, that's a cruel thing to say!' His tone sharpened with a sudden edge of anger. 'I respect you too much to treat you like that.'

She did not believe him for one moment. How could he feel anything for her when he was still presumably

85

seeing Riva? He was lying. He had no respect for her at all. 'I didn't expect sexual harassment when I agreed to work for you,' she spat bitterly.

'Sexual harassment?' The glitter in his eyes turned to shards of ice, his arms around her like bands of iron. 'If that's what I'd planned then you'd know about it. I consider I treat you like a lady.'

'Then let me go,' she demanded fiercely. 'No lady likes to feel that she's being forced into anything.'

'I've never forced you, Hannah, and you know it.' Rage added strength to his words. 'But perhaps I ought to show you what it's like to be kissed against your will.' His smile was cold and brutal, but nothing like as cruel as the hardness of his mouth as it crushed her lips. Faintness stole over Hannah as electric tension joined pleasure, joined fear. Treetops began to spin as her breath caught in her throat and she tried in vain to escape. Jordan was using her to drive out his anger, her lips ground mercilessly back against her teeth, the kiss lasting for ever, until he finally, savagely, thrust her away from him, his breathing ragged and heavy, his eyes masked so that she no longer knew what he was thinking.

At the same moment there was a stir in the crowd and Daniel pushed through the smiling, chattering people towards them. With an effort Hannah pulled herself together. She must not let her son see that there was anything wrong, although her whole body felt as though there wasn't enough strength in it to last her through the rest of the day.

'Did you see them?' he asked excitedly. 'Did you see the monkey pouring the tea? Isn't he clever?'

He monopolised the conversation for the rest of the day, running excitedly from one enclosure to another, not seeming to notice that his mother and Mr Quest were barely speaking to each other. Strangely, Hannah felt more conscious of Jordan than ever before. That punishing kiss, instead of repulsing her, had created more awareness and consequently more tension.

They had sandwiches for their lunch in the tea-rooms, and Jordan ate heartily, but Hannah scarcely ate a thing, and when Daniel's feet began to drag she was glad of the excuse to suggest they go home. She had spent almost two whole days in Jordan's company, and it was more than enough. She wanted to return to her flat, she wanted to relax and be herself and try to put out of her mind all the things that had happened this weekend.

Jordan's knuckles were white on the wheel, his whole body tense and filled with suppressed anger. The journey was long and silent and intolerable. Daniel had fallen asleep, and the tension built up and up until Hannah felt ready to scream. When Jordan pulled up outside the old Victorian house he lifted Daniel out and carried him upstairs, but the instant he put the child down he turned abruptly and left. Not one word was spoken between them.

Hannah let him go, but she felt unhappy about the situation. She had not wanted to cause a rift. All she had been trying to do was tell him that he was pushing for too much too soon. He had not really sexually harassed her—she should not have said that, it had been wrong and cruel. But no more cruel than his sadistic kiss, said a tiny voice inside her. She touched her fingers experimentally to her mouth and took a look at herself in the mirror. She was appalled to see how swollen her lips were, her eyes like deep shadowy pools in a face that was deathly pale.

Her actions were automatic as she made Daniel's supper and bathed him and put him to bed, before taking a bath herself. She lay in the warm scented water and thought of Jordan, thought of the effect he had on her body, and the fact that she still had to go to work for him tomorrow. Would the tension be too much to handle? Would it be best if she handed in her notice? This was the last thing she wanted to do, the money he paid her was too valuable, but if the strain persisted it might be her only choice.

Monday in the office was every bit as bad as Hannah had feared. When she'd first gone to work for Jordan he had treated her like a human machine, and this was how it was again. He worked her harder than ever before, seeming not to see her as a person, never once looking directly at her.

Hannah gritted her teeth and got on with it. If that was the way he wanted to play things, so be it. She had never encouraged him, she had always made it very clear that she still loved Roger. The fact that he was managing to get through her defences was a problem, but not an insurmountable one. She was used to wrapping her feelings in ice and getting on with her life.

When Riva March came into the office shortly before one Hannah gave an inward groan. This was one person she could do without seeing. 'Shall I ring Mr Quest through that you're here?' she asked, when the girl came to a halt directly in front of her desk.

'I want a word with you first,' came the cutting reply. 'Didn't I make it clear that Jordan belongs to me?'

He *belonged* to her? Like a possession? Hannah somehow doubted that Jordan belonged to anyone. He struck her as being his own man, doing whatever he wanted when he wanted. He enjoyed his freedom too much to be tied down to any one woman. Riva suited his purpose sometimes, but not always. And the girl must be pretty thick-skinned not to suspect this. But whatever the case, he was welcome to her. She managed a polite smile. 'You made it perfectly clear,' she agreed.

'But it was you he was out with over the weekend? Isn't that right?'

Hannah saw no reason to lie, and nodded.

'I thought as much.' The girl's green eyes glittered with pure hatred, making Hannah shudder. 'How did you persuade him to ask you?'

'I didn't do anything,' Hannah informed her tightly. 'Jordan invited and I accepted, it's as simple as that.' Let the girl make of it what she liked.

'Jordan usually takes me out on a Saturday night. He wouldn't ask you unless you made up to him,' spat the girl savagely. 'If it's a rich husband you're after you're barking up the wrong tree. Jordan isn't the marrying type. He's happy with his life the way it is—and I'm happy to be a part of it. I'm not going to let you or anyone else come between us!' Flames of fury were dancing from her eyes, her shapely body taut with anger.

'I think,' said Hannah, keeping her voice level with great difficulty, 'that what Jordan does is up to him. But if it will please you, I doubt whether he'll ask me out again.'

Riva's bright red lips drew back in a cat-like smile. 'I'm not surprised you failed to please him. You're really not his type. I wonder he wasted his time on you.'

Her tone hurt, but Hannah allowed the glimmer of a smile. What would the blonde say if she knew that she had been the one to do the rejecting? 'I'll tell Mr Quest you're here,' she said.

His deep, resonant voice barked into the phone when Hannah rang through, but despite his treatment of her it still had the power to quiver along her nerves.

'Miss March is here,' she said coolly.

'Send her in, Mrs Carpenter, and bring along two coffees as well.'

The 'Mrs Carpenter' hurt, and when she took in their drinks a little while later it hurt still more to see Riva March withdrawing from his arms, a 'cat who'd stolen the cream' smile on her face.

'Thank you, Mrs Carpenter, just put them down there, and see to it that I'm not disturbed for the next hour,' Jordan ordered.

Hannah clenched her teeth, and although she did not want to look at him their eyes somehow met. She felt a tingle start from the top of her spine and run all the way down her back. There was challenge in his eyes—it was as if he was testing her, trying to see what effect his relationship with Riva had on her. For a stormy few seconds she held his gaze, but was determined not to give anything away. She eyed him quite coolly and calmly, then swung on her heel and left the room.

It was well over an hour before his door opened again, and during that time Hannah immersed herself in her work, trying not to think about Jordan, trying to concentrate totally on the job in hand. It was almost impossible. She kept wondering what they were doing. Although it was lunchtime she had no appetite for her own sandwiches, and it was most unusual for Jordan not to go out, or at least send for some sandwiches himself. It was obvious he was having lunch of an entirely different kind.

Hannah's eyes followed them across the room, then she wished she hadn't been watching when Riva put her arms around his neck and gave him a lingering goodbye kiss. 'I'll see you tonight, Jordan darling,' she purred.

His reply was too low for Hannah to hear, but there was a pleased smile on his face when he made his way back into his own office.

Half-past four could not come quickly enough for Hannah. Why, when she did not want Jordan herself, was she fuelled with jealousy because he was seeing another woman? It did not make sense. Her thoughts were still full of Jordan and Riva when she walked out of the building, and she did not see the man standing outside until she almost cannoned into him. 'Drew!' she exclaimed in surprise. 'What are you doing here?'

'Waiting for you,' came the startling reply.

'Me?' she frowned. 'What do you want with me?'

He grinned. 'I want to take you out. I don't see why my brother should have all the fun.'

'Oh, Drew, I can't,' she said sorrowfully. 'I have my son to look after.'

'You managed to find someone to watch him when you went out with Jordan,' he pointed out.

'Yes,' she admitted ruefully, 'but—well, I can't do that too often.'

'Can't or won't?' he asked. 'Come on, Hannah, you're not being fair. Find yourself a baby-sitter and we'll paint the town red.'

His irrepressible grin was very much in evidence, and Hannah could not help smiling at his enthusiasm. Actually she thought she might like to go out with him. He was good fun, he made her laugh and feel carefree. She did not feel any pressures as she did with Jordan. 'Perhaps one day,' she agreed.

But 'one day' was not good enough for Drew. 'How about tomorrow? Come on, Hannah, be a sport. We'll go to Shady's nightclub. You'll like it there. They have a casino where we can——'

'No, Drew,' interrupted Hannah firmly. 'I don't have money to throw away—and nor do you now you're out of work.'

He grinned cheekily. 'I will have soon.'

'You've got another job?' she asked, pleased.

'No, I haven't, and I don't need one,' he told her grandly. 'I'm about to inherit a fortune. I'm going to be a rich man, Hannah. I need never work again. So how about it—are you going to come out with me tomorrow night?'

Still she shook her head. 'I don't think so. A casino isn't the sort of place I'd enjoy.'

'Then what do you enjoy? I'll take you for a meal, anything, so long as you'll come out with me. You're surely not waiting for Jordan to ask you again? He's hardly likely to do that, he spends most of his spare time with Riva March—you must have met her?'

Hannah nodded. 'We've met,' she answered crisply.

'And you're no more enamoured of her than I am,' he concluded. 'But my dear brother thinks very differently. He's been going out with her for simply ages. I wouldn't be surprised if a wedding wasn't on the cards.'

Hannah felt her heart stop and miss a beat. It was as she had thought. But why had Jordan lied? 'He told me he didn't think very much of her,' she said.

'He's always saying that,' Drew told her easily, 'but he still goes on seeing her. Have you changed your mind now? Will you let me take you out?'

But Hannah's answer was still no. She wanted neither of these Quest brothers to become a part of her life.

'At least let me take you home,' he said.

Drew met her from the office the following two afternoons. Always he asked her to go out with him, and always she refused. Although she was tempted she had a feeling he might get serious, and that was the last thing she wanted.

Yvonne Howard was intrigued by yet another man in her neighbour's life, and did not altogether believe Hannah when she told her that Drew was nothing more than a friend. She had tried to pump her about what had gone wrong with Jordan, but Hannah had kept silent. She was never one to discuss her problems with other people, preferring to keep her private affairs private.

Jordan still continued to treat her like a robot, never letting her know by even the blink of an eyelid what his feelings were. Until Thursday! Without Hannah being aware of it he left the office building a few seconds after her, and when he saw her stepping into his brother's car, her face wreathed in smiles, his expression turned to one of fury. He yanked the door open and caught hold of her arm.

'What the hell is all this about?' he demanded loudly.

'I'm giving Hannah a lift home, that's what,' answered Drew. 'And it's none of your business.'

Jordan's frown was deep and livid. 'How long has this been going on?' And still he did not let Hannah go.

'There's nothing going on, old boy,' retorted Drew. 'I feel sorry for Hannah having to walk, it's as simple as that. If you weren't so busy making your millions you'd probably have seen for yourself that she has no car.'

'Less of the lip, Drew,' snarled Jordan, and to Hannah, 'Get out, I'll take you.'

She felt like a mouse being fought over by two birds of prey, not knowing which way to turn.

'I said, get out!' he rasped when she hesitated, and without more ado he hauled her wholesale out of the car. 'Now get going,' he rapped at Drew, 'and I don't want you pestering Hannah again. Is that clear?'

'He wasn't pestering me,' protested Hannah. 'He was simply being kind.'

'Shut up!' Jordan thrust savagely.

Drew frowned and began to get out of his car to defend her, but Hannah said quickly, 'Please, Drew, it's all right. You'd better go.'

'If he so much as lays a finger on you, I'll——'

'Jordan won't hurt me,' she said softly, hoping it was true.

'Now,' said Jordan, marching her to his car, 'I think you have some explaining to do.'

'I don't think so,' she said tightly, sliding reluctantly inside as he opened the door. 'What I do is none of your business.'

'It's very much my business when it concerns you and my brother,' he retorted. He slammed the door and strode round to the other side, leaping in and starting the engine. 'Charming he might be, but he's far too weak for someone like you.' He let in the clutch and the car shot forward. 'How long has this been going on?'

Hannah shrugged. 'Just this week.'

A muscle tensed in his jaw. 'And knowing Drew I can't believe he'd settle for something as simple as giving you a lift home. How much time do you spend together?'

'None!' exclaimed Hannah.

'I don't believe you.'

She lifted her shoulders. 'It's true, whether you believe it or not. He has asked me out, I'll admit that, but I've never gone. You know how I feel about leaving Daniel.'

'You mean that if it wasn't for your son you might have accepted his invitation?' His thick brows beetled over eyes that were thunderously dark and angrily suspicious. 'Are my first misgivings confirmed? Do you prefer him to me?'

'I prefer no one,' she protested. 'I admit I find Drew very easy to get on with. He accepts me as I am and doesn't want anything that I'm not prepared to give. But I'm not ready for another relationship, not with Drew, you or anyone. Why don't you believe me?'

She stole a glance at his grim profile as he negotiated an island, his gear-changes quick and jerky, nothing at all like his normal smooth, relaxed style of driving. The taut angles of his face made her shiver, yet she did not see why he should be so viciously angry. He was acting like a jealous man, which did not entirely add up when all he wanted from her was her body.

'Because that's not the way it looks.' He finally answered her question. 'When you're with me you hold something back, but with my brother you're a different person. I asked you this before, is he the type you prefer?'

Hannah shook her head, her lips twisted in exasperation. 'There is no type. I'm happy the way I am, just me and Danny.'

'And your memories,' he thrust caustically.

She shrugged. 'Is that a sin?'

'It's unhealthy.'

'I'm very loyal to the man I love.' She wished he would understand, wished he would accept that she was fighting a hard battle. When you belonged body and soul to a man it was difficult to let go of the memories.

Jordan slammed the brakes on so suddenly outside the flats that she was jerked forward, but there was no hint of an apology, and Hannah quickly unfastened her seatbelt and scrambled out.

Her legs were trembling as she made her way upstairs and she prayed Yvonne had not noticed Jordan's car. She did not want to have to answer questions about the two brothers. But her prayers were in vain.

'Wasn't that Jordan who dropped you off?' asked her neighbour at once.

Hannah nodded.

'So what's going on? Honestly, Hannah, I'm dying of curiosity, and you never tell me a thing!'

'There's nothing to tell.' Hannah shrugged. 'Jordan was coming this way and gave me a lift, that's all.'

'That's all?' There was a knowing smile on the older woman's face. 'You must have patched up your differences—I'm so pleased. He's perfect for you.'

Hannah shook her head. 'Yvonne, you know as well as I do that I don't want another man in my life. Jordan's my boss and that's all there is to it. Besides, he has a girlfriend. Come on, Danny, we must let Mrs Howard go to work.'

Yvonne looked disappointed, but wisely kept silent. Daniel, however, had no such compunction. 'Why didn't you ask Mr Quest to come in, Mummy? He could play with my trains. It's been ages since I saw him.'

'Mr Quest is a very busy man, Danny, I've told you that before.'

'I think you don't like him any more.'

Hannah was astounded that he had reached such a decision.

'You won't let me talk about him,' Daniel went on. 'You always start talking about something else.'

'That's true, Danny,' she said quietly, 'but it's not because I don't like him, it's because he has no part to play in our lives. I don't want you getting too fond of him.'

'Won't he ever take us out again?'

'No, I don't think so.'

'That's not fair! I love him, I want him to come and play with me. He's lots of fun. Don't you love him, Mummy?'

Hannah felt a surge of warmth go through her at so candid a question. Her feelings for Jordan were certainly not love, but she did not know what they were. A strong liking perhaps, a physical attraction, but that was about all.

'Of course I don't love him,' she said. 'I love your daddy.'

'But Daddy's not here any more.' A tear traced a course down his cheek. 'How can you love him when he's not here? I want a new daddy, I want Mr Quest to be my daddy!'

She gathered Daniel into her arms. 'Darling, that's not possible and you know it. Please don't cry. Perhaps one day I'll find another man to love, but not yet. I still love your daddy too much.'

He struggled free and ran into his room, and Hannah knew it was best to leave him. She did not like to see him upset, but there was little or nothing she could do about it. She could not love Jordan Quest to order. And besides, he didn't love her, it was all a game he was playing. Any sort of union had to be a two-way affair.

The next morning Jordan called her into his office the moment she arrived. 'I've been talking to Drew,' he said without preamble. 'He told me that he can't get anywhere with you—*even though he's tried*.' These last words were hissed through closed teeth.

She eyed him coolly. 'You'll accept his word though you wouldn't accept mine? Is that what you're trying to tell me? I don't find that very flattering.'

'He's nearer your age, he's good-looking, he's easy-going—what was I to think?'

'Who knows what goes on in a mind like yours?' she retaliated sharply.

'He also mentioned that he's told you about his inheritance.'

She nodded.

'That was an unwise thing for him to do.'

'Why?' she frowned. 'Because you think I might find him more interesting now that he's wealthy in his own right?' It was just the sort of conclusion he would draw.

Jordan snorted derisively. 'I don't think you'd be that foolish, but it's wrong of Drew to go around telling people something that's not strictly true.'

'You mean there is no inheritance?' queried Hannah.

'Oh, yes,' he confirmed, 'but it's not money as Drew presumes, it's property—a whole estate, in fact. And if he thinks he can sell it to make money so that he won't have to work again, he's mistaken.'

There was a toughness to his tone that made Hannah look at him in surprise. 'Can you stop him?' she asked.

'I'm his trustee until he's thirty—although he doesn't know that yet. The will is being read tomorrow. My aunt loved him dearly despite his reckless ways, and I think she hoped the responsibility would be the making of him. I personally have my doubts.'

The phone rang at that moment, making further conversation impossible, and Hannah returned to her own office. She could not help wondering what Drew would say when he discovered that Jordan was his trustee and there was no actual money.

They were so different, these two brothers, their outlook on life at complete odds to one another. Drew would make a good friend, she knew that, a cheerful companion to lift her out of herself and make her laugh. Jordan, on the other hand, was beginning to get through to both the emotional and physical side of her. There were times when she found herself thinking about him and not Roger, and she felt very guilty when she did so. It still seemed far too soon to show an interest in another man. She had never thought that she would, had never wanted to; it was happening against her will.

Saturday was the same as any other Saturday: shopping, washing, cleaning, ironing. Hannah always tried to do all her work in one day so that she could devote the whole of Sunday to Daniel. They usually managed to go out somewhere, even if it was only a bus ride to a local beauty spot. But on Sunday morning he awoke complaining of a sore throat and he seemed to be running a temperature, so she gave him some aspirin and kept him in bed.

On Monday he was no better, and she sent for the doctor, who diagnosed tonsillitis and prescribed a course of antibiotics. She telephoned Jordan and told him that she would not be at work until he was better. It was the first time she had ever needed to take time off.

When the doorbell rang on Monday evening the last person she expected to see was Jordan.

'Aren't you going to ask me in?' he asked with a quirk to his lips.

'I'm sorry, you surprised me.' More than surprised her, in fact. She could not think what he was doing here.

'I've come to see how the invalid is.' He followed her into the tiny living-room, and at once she felt his presence filling it. He was wearing white drill trousers and a yellow half-sleeved shirt and looked totally different from the hard-faced man who had ignored her for most of the week. Her heart began to beat abnormally fast and she found it difficult to take her eyes off him. It was crazy, the effect he was beginning to have on her.

'Who's that?' Daniel's voice came from out of his bedroom.

'You'd better go in,' said Hannah. 'He'll be delighted to see you, he's done nothing but talk about you since last weekend. You've made quite an impression.'

'I wish I'd made the same impression on his mother.' Jordan's tone was low and sensual, his eyes on hers, and Hannah felt a sudden warmth rush through her.

'Mummy, is that Mr Quest?'

The spell was broken, thank goodness, and Jordan turned away, but not before he had touched his fingers to her cheek. It probably meant nothing to him, it was merely a way of saying that he had got over his anger and was prepared to be friends again. But to what extent? What did he expect of her? She was still not ready to give her all to him, even though he was beginning to mean more to her than any other man since Roger.

She followed him to Daniel's room, watching from the doorway as he handed her son a flat parcel. Danny's fingers trembled in his eagerness to open it.

It was a book. Jordan could not have bought him anything better; Daniel loved reading. A book about wild animals, their habitat, their eating habits, how they brought up their young, written in a language simple enough for him to understand and beautifully illustrated.

'Thank you, Mr Quest, thank you!' breathed Daniel. 'Look, Mummy, isn't it lovely?'

Moving over to the bed, standing so close to Jordan that she could feel the warmth of him and smell the faint tang of his aftershave, Hannah looked down at the open page and smiled and nodded. 'It's very nice, Danny.'

But she was more aware of the man at her side than the pictures in the book.

'I love animals,' went on Daniel enthusiastically. 'I used to help my daddy around the farm. We had a dog then, and a cat, but Mummy says I can't have one now because we have no garden.'

Jordan nodded gravely. 'Your mummy's right, Danny—pets need lots of exercise. It wouldn't be fair to keep them shut up indoors all the time.'

'I wish I lived in your house with your big garden,' added Daniel. 'There'd be lots of room then.'

'Danny!' choked Hannah, mortified by his frankness, but terrified too that he might say something even more embarrassing.

'It's all right,' smiled Jordan.

'No, it's not all right,' she said sharply. 'He never speaks like this to anyone else.'

'I guess Danny and I understand each other.'

'I think you encourage him to be rude,' she snapped.

'Not intentionally, Hannah. I would never do that. I respect your authority and compliment you on a very well-mannered little boy. He's done nothing wrong.'

'He's spoken out of turn.'

'If you repress him he'll be an introvert. There's nothing wrong in stating his opinion.'

Daniel was watching them both with interest, not altogether sure what was going on, but intrigued to see his mother arguing with Mr Quest.

'Look at your book for a few minutes, Danny,' Hannah said, kissing his brow, 'and then go to sleep.'

She walked out of the room, hoping Jordan would take the hint and follow. He stayed a moment longer; she heard the low murmur of their voices and envied how easily Danny got on with Jordan. He had no hang-ups about letting anyone else into his life. How she wished she could accept this man so freely!

When Jordan joined her she was standing at the window looking down into the street. He came into the room so quietly that she was not aware of him until he spoke her name softly over her shoulder.

She turned and looked at him without a trace of a smile, although inside she felt the full power of his magnetism. He *was* like a magnet, she thought, pulling her inexorably towards him even though she did her best to resist. Her chin lifted. 'I'd appreciate it if you didn't tell me how to bring up my child,' she said. 'It was very kind of you to bring that book, but now Daniel needs his rest, so if you wouldn't mind . . .' She walked over to the door and opened it.

Jordan followed. He took the door out of her hand and closed it again. 'You don't get rid of me that easily,' he told her.

Hannah felt a quick spurt of annoyance. 'I thought you came to see Daniel?'

'That was my excuse.'

Meaning he wanted to see her! Hannah controlled a sigh and, turning back into the room, she sat down. Jordan took the other easy chair, his long legs stretched out in front. He looked relaxed and perfectly at home, even though the room had none of the comforts he was used to.

'Are you worried because I'm not able to do your work?' she asked pertly.

A smile curved his lips. 'Not at all. I have an entirely different proposition to put to you.'

Hannah sat up and looked at him suspiciously.

'But first let me tell you about the estate my aunt left Drew.' He sat forward, his elbows resting on his thighs, his hands outstretched ready to add emphasis to his words. 'As I said, my brother's far too irresponsible to run it himself. In fact, if it weren't for my aunt stipulating that it must be kept in the family, he'd sell tomorrow. The estate has actually been in the Quest family for over three hundred years. It would be criminal to let it go— perhaps to someone who would want to develop in a way that would be completely out of character.'

'But what's it got to do with me?' asked Hannah, still feeling totally confused.

'I'm coming to that,' he assured her. 'Drew, as you might expect, is not at all pleased that I've been made his trustee. We've had some very sharp words about it. He seems to think that even though he can't sell the estate he can live in the Hall, collect the rents, and provide himself with a comfortable income. It wouldn't work out like that.'

Hannah remained silent. She still could not see what part she had to play in any of this.

'You see, my aunt hasn't been well these last few years, and in consequence the estate has been badly neglected— rents not rising in line with inflation, rents not even collected, maintenance work on the cottages not done. The whole community is really in a very sad state.'

'So who's going to look after it? Who's going to see that all this work is done?' asked Hannah. He was right, it wasn't the sort of thing Drew would be capable of handling. Drew didn't like anything that resembled hard work.

'I am,' said Jordan, much to her surprise. 'Obviously I shall make Drew a reasonable allowance just as soon as it begins to get back on its feet. And if and when he ever shows signs of maturity then he can take over.'

'But you're already very busy running your own company.'

He dismissed her protest airily. 'My company will run itself for the time being. I have very efficient managers, as you know. And I shall keep in regular touch. I don't foresee any problems.'

'Where is this estate?' she asked.

'In Derbyshire, not far from where my parents live. Right out in the countryside. It will suit you and Danny perfectly.'

Her frown reappeared. 'Me and Danny? What are you talking about?'

'I want you there with me, Hannah. I want you to marry me and live there as my wife.'

CHAPTER SEVEN

HANNAH did not realise that she had stopped breathing until her head began to spin. She gulped air into her tortured lungs and stared at Jordan as though he were a ghost. 'You can't be serious?'

'I assure you I am.'

'But—but you don't love me,' she stammered. And hadn't Drew said he was going to marry Riva?

'Neither do you love me, but we're both in need of a partner, and I can think of no better excuse.'

Hannah continued to look at him in wide-eyed disbelief. 'How can you say that?' she whispered huskily, her mouth so dry she felt as if she had been in the desert for days without water.

'It's simple. Let me list all the "for"'s. Number one, I find you very, very attractive and far less irritating than most women I know.'

Did that include Riva? she wondered.

'Secondly, Daniel and I get on well together—it's a mutual admiration in that respect. He's a fine boy. Thirdly, although you need a man in your life you're not prepared to love again, which suits me fine because I don't believe in love either. Call it a business arrangement if you like, because I'll need you to help me run the estate. Or a marriage of convenience. Whatever, it's one that will suit us both admirably.'

Hannah felt as though she was going to pass out. It was a wildly fanciful suggestion. How could he even think it would work? She closed her eyes and tried to regulate her breathing, and the next thing she knew Jordan was touching her shoulder.

'Hannah, look at me. Are you all right?'

She dragged open her eyes and took a grateful sip of the water he offered.

'I didn't realise it would be quite such a shock,' he murmured.

'What did you think,' she scorned, 'that I'd jump for joy and accept straight away?' She took the glass from him and gulped down the rest of the contents. 'It's ludicrous! I can't possibly consider it. And besides, I'm not sure that I entirely agree with your taking the estate away from Drew so completely. It seems most unfair.'

'It's the only logical solution,' he said. 'I daren't let Drew loose there, it would sink even deeper into the quagmire. And as far as you and I are concerned it's a very practical arrangement,' he told her firmly. 'Think of the advantages. You'd have no more money worries, for a start, you'd be living back out in the country, which can only be good for Daniel, and you'd also be giving the boy the father he desperately needs. To say nothing of your own needs. It's a perfect solution.'

'And what would you get out of it?' she asked, wondering what he thought her needs were.

'A ready-made family, although I'm not saying I wouldn't like children of my own one day. A beautiful, charming wife, an efficient secretary. The estate manager who looked after things for my aunt hasn't kept the books properly for years. There's so much work to be done.'

'I could work for you without marrying you,' she pointed out.

'Agreed, but it's too far to travel, you'd still need to live at the Hall. And you're such a sensitive little person,'

Jordan added caustically, 'that you'd be sure to worry what people might say.'

'And you think I'd marry you for that reason?' Her chin was high now, her blue eyes coldly defensive.

'I know you wouldn't do that, Hannah, but I know you're not entirely immune to me either. I know it's only your misguided sense of loyalty that makes you hold back.'

'Would you—would you—expect me to sleep with you?' she asked faintly, her face colouring as she posed the question, but it was something that needed to be said if she was to consider his suggestion, and she had to admit that it made a lot of sense.

'Naturally.' His lips quirked as he saw the colour deepen in her cheeks. 'But I wouldn't rush you. On the other hand, I wouldn't be prepared to wait for ever,' he added pointedly. 'Think about my proposal, Hannah. I'll call in again tomorrow evening. Perhaps by then Daniel will be feeling better and you'll be able to see what he thinks about it.'

'No!' said Hannah at once, hotly and loudly, 'I won't have Danny involved—that's blackmail. He already thinks the world of you, and——'

'There you are, then,' he broke in with a smile, 'that's half the battle over.'

Hannah realised she had let her tongue run away with her and cursed beneath her breath. 'I'll give you your answer tomorrow, Mr Quest. Please go now.'

'*Mr Quest?*' A frown deepened the creases in his brow and his voice hardened. 'What is this? Have you already made up your mind?' He rose to his feet and towered over her. 'If so, tell me now. I have no wish to lie awake half the night hoping in vain.'

'It's all a game to you, isn't it?' she snapped, springing up as well. 'You want a wife in name only, an image of respectability, while you carry on and bed Riva March and any other female who takes your fancy!'

Jordan's eyes narrowed as he hissed chillingly, 'Is that honestly what you think I'd do?'

'I'm sure of it,' she spat.

'Then let me spell it out to you, Miss Suspicious Mind. Once we were married I would be completely faithful. The only person I'd sleep with would be you. As I said before, I'd give you time, but if I thought it was too long in coming——' his eyes roved purposefully over her quivering body '—then I might not be quite so patient.'

It shamed Hannah that her pulses leapt in response, that her body betrayed her when she wanted nothing to do with him—and her heightened colour unfortunately gave her away.

'But I have no doubt that you wouldn't keep me waiting very long,' he taunted. Without warning he reached out and pulled her against him, his mouth capturing hers before she could even think about pulling free.

It was no punishing kiss this time—it was designed to arouse her senses and persuade her in no small way that she found him far more attractive than she was admitting. His mouth moved with calculated expertise over hers, nibbling gently the soft fullness of her lower lip, his tongue probing and exciting, his hands a burning caress.

Hannah knew she was lost the moment he touched her. Her senses spun until she was no longer capable of coherent thought. She clung urgently to Jordan, feeling the strength of silken muscle beneath her fingertips, the pulsating hardness of his body against hers, having no idea how long the kiss lasted, coming to her senses only when Daniel's voice broke into her tormented mind.

'Mummy, has Mr Quest gone?'

She tried to wrench herself free, horrified that she had responded so freely and easily. 'Not yet, darling.' Even her voice was shaky and weak.

Jordan smiled tenderly and stroked a warm finger down her trembling cheek. 'Tell him you're going to marry me.'

'I can't,' she whispered chokingly.

'Can't tell him, or can't marry me?' he wondered, still teasing her with fingers that were altogether too sensual.

Hannah closed her eyes and let her thoughts run free. Accepting Jordan's proposal actually made a lot of sense. Daniel was desperately in need of a father figure, there was no doubt about it, and as he loved Jordan already she knew he wouldn't object. It was in fact his dearest wish. If he had any idea what Jordan was saying to her now he would be out of bed like a shot, adding his persuasion to Jordan's.

She knew she would never love another man as she had loved Roger, nevertheless she did feel a certain kind of love for Jordan, even though she had not admitted it even to herself up until this moment! It was a heart-stopping discovery. She had fought strongly against developing any kind of feelings, but they had crept up on her unwittingly, and now she was powerless to do anything about it.

'I'm still waiting, Hannah.' Jordan's lips brushed hers again, sending a fresh shiver of emotions through her already nerveless limbs.

She swallowed hard and licked suddenly dry lips. 'I— I think my answer is—yes. I will—marry you, Jordan.'

It should have been a joyous moment, but instead tears welled and trickled down her cheeks.

There was a moment's tension in him before he smiled and brushed away her tears with gentle thumbs. 'Hannah, it isn't anything to cry about. You won't regret this, I promise you. Let's go and tell Daniel.'

The days that followed were not easy ones. Under normal circumstances they should have been some of the happiest in Hannah's life, but the circumstances were anything but normal, and apart from Daniel, who was delirious with excitement, and her parents who had been highly delighted when she phoned and gave them her news, no one else seemed to think that she was doing the right thing.

The first person to warn her off Jordan was Drew. He came to see her at the flat the very next day, his face mottled red with anger and disbelief. 'Tell me it's not true that you're going to marry my brother?' he demanded.

'I'm afraid it is true,' Hannah said softly.

He swore viciously and slammed his fist on to the edge of a chair. 'But why? Why are you marrying him? I can't believe that you love him, and he as sure as hell doesn't love you.'

'I do love him,' she whispered.

Drew snorted and paced across the room. 'Since when?'

'Since yesterday, I suppose,' she told him reluctantly. 'At least, that's when I discovered it.'

'With a little help from my brother, I've no doubt,' he sneered. 'I think you're making a big mistake, Hannah, but what's just as galling is the fact that you're going to live at the Hall. You're going to live in *my* property! I can't believe that Aunt Kate made Jordan my trustee. Didn't she think I was capable of running the estate?'

'I'm sorry, Drew,' said Hannah softly, 'and if it's any consolation, I feel as guilty as anything about that part of it. But it's only until Jordan gets it on its feet again, and then he'll hand it over to you. He's really doing you a favour.'

'Maybe,' he muttered sullenly.

It was the first time Hannah had seen Drew anything but laughing and carefree and happy, and really she couldn't blame him. The estate was obviously the real issue, not the fact that she was marrying his brother, and she could understand his very real hurt. But she also knew that he was not yet capable of running it himself. For his age he was very immature; all he was concerned about was having a good time, and he saw the estate as another way of getting money to do it. It was a shame. He was such a nice boy. She really did feel sorry for him.

Hannah's next warning came from Riva on the day she went back to work following Daniel's attack of tonsillitis. The girl came storming into her office almost within minutes of Hannah arriving.

'I don't know how you've managed it,' she raged, her face ugly with anger, 'but I do know one thing—it won't last. Nor will Jordan be true to you. Your marriage won't stop him seeing me!'

This was one of Hannah's fears too, despite his avowal of loyalty, but she had no intention of letting the blonde siren know that. 'You're mistaken,' she smiled confidently. 'Jordan and I are deeply in love.'

Riva's eyes narrowed suspiciously. 'He's actually told you that he loves you?'

'Of course,' Hannah lied.

'Jordan always told me he didn't believe in love,' Riva frowned.

Hannah shrugged. 'He's obviously changed his mind. Perhaps he was waiting for the right girl to come along?'

'Maybe you were the one who did the persuading,' sneered Riva, 'but he'll come to his senses, you just wait and see. He'll soon realise that a snivelling kid and a frigid bitch who's still in love with her dead husband are no comparison to the sort of pleasures he gets from me!'

Hannah flinched at her harsh words and felt the sharp sting of tears, but she tossed her head and held them back. 'How dare you speak to me like that? Jordan loves my son and Daniel loves Jordan. We're going to be very happy.' And how dared Jordan tell Riva about Roger! That hurt more than Riva's caustic comments.

'Of course we're going to be happy.' Jordan appeared from nowhere and put his arm about Hannah's shoulders, and she wondered with a sinking heart how much of the conversation he had heard.

Riva muttered something and left the office, and Jordan released Hannah instantly. 'I'm sorry she subjected you to that,' he said. 'It was most unbecoming of her.'

Hannah shrugged, more disappointed that he had let her go than concerned about Riva. Those few seconds' contact had quickened every one of her senses, and she wondered how long she would last without letting him know how deeply she felt.

The day after she promised to marry him she had woken with a lovely warm feeling inside her, with a sense of relief. It would be good to have a man to make the decisions, to assume some of the responsibility for

Daniel, to share her bed! Her thoughts had halted at this stage. There would be no nuptial bed—it would be wrong to share with a man who did not love her. She had made a silent vow there and then that until Jordan declared his love she would sleep alone. Even if it meant for ever!

'And it was very brave of you to lie and say that we loved each other,' Jordan went on. 'You made it sound very convincing.'

Swift, guilty colour reddened Hannah's cheeks and she turned away. 'I had to say something to put her in her place,' she muttered.

'I thought there might have been an element of truth in it?' he questioned softly. He was behind her, his mouth close to her ear, his breath warm on her cheek.

'None at all,' she retorted sharply.

'That's a pity. I really would have liked to start married life without competing with Roger.'

She turned at that, her blue eyes dancing fire. 'You had no right telling Riva how I felt about him. It was a despicable thing to do!'

'I didn't tell her,' he said, his lips tightening. 'It was a calculated guess.'

'And I'm expected to believe that?' Hannah asked scornfully. 'Really, Jordan, what sort of an idiot do you take me for?'

'You're no idiot, Hannah. I wouldn't be marrying you if you were. And by the way, don't make any plans for Sunday, because I'm taking you to see my parents. I think it only right that they should meet you before the wedding.'

Meet his parents! Hannah swallowed a sudden hard lump in her throat. 'Have you—have you—fixed the date?' she asked haltingly. This was the first time she had seen Jordan since the night she had agreed to marry him. She had expected him to call at the flat again, but he never had. And why should he when it had been no ordinary proposal? she asked herself frequently. Why should he bother with such niceties? And yet his neglect hurt. After discovering she was in love with him she had dearly wanted to spend more time with him. Even Daniel had asked where he was, and it had been difficult thinking up excuses to keep him satisfied.

She had arrived at the office this morning with her heart thumping and every nerve on red alert, and when Riva appeared before she had had time to speak with him she could have screamed. And now she was waiting to hear when they were going to get married!

'A week today at eleven in the register office,' Jordan answered, adding cynically, 'I thought a church wedding would be a mockery, considering the way we feel about each other.'

Hannah felt disappointed, and yet he was right. Besides, she and Roger had had a white church wedding, and it would feel disloyal to do it all over again with someone else. 'You're not giving me much time,' she protested.

'To do what?' he asked with a frown. 'Buy yourself a new dress? Does it take that long? Everything else has been taken care of.'

'I was thinking about my flat. I——'

'I've already seen your landlord,' he cut in abruptly. 'You have nothing to worry about.'

Hannah could not believe that he had made all these arrangements without consulting her. It was all so different from when she and Roger had got married. Half the excitement had been in planning and organising things together. Now there was none of that. A chill crept over her, and she wondered whether she ought to back out now while she still had the chance.

'I suggest we catch up on some work.' Jordan's crisp tone interrupted her thoughts. 'Melanie has been doing her best, but she's not half so efficient as you.'

For the rest of the week he worked her like a slave. He wanted every loose end tied up before their wedding and subsequent move to Derbyshire. Every manager had to be briefed, every problem solved, every letter answered. There was no time for personal conversation, no time for intimacies. He worked late each evening, piling up the work for when Hannah arrived the next day.

On Friday afternoon he told her he would be at the office all day on Saturday too, but he would pick her and Daniel up at eleven on Sunday for their visit to his parents.

Hannah was dreading this visit almost as much as she was dreading the wedding. What if they didn't like her? What if they didn't approve? They were going to live so close, it was obvious they would be seeing them quite frequently. Jordan had told her nothing about them, so she really had no idea what to expect.

'Have you bought your dress yet?' he asked suddenly, and when Hannah shook her head he pushed a slip of paper into her hand. 'Get yourself and Daniel something nice.'

It was a cheque for an amount that made Hannah's eyes widen, and she was about to refuse when she realised that on Monday she would be his wife, so why not use his money? She had been worrying how she would find enough for a suitable outfit, and now her problem was solved.

'Thank you,' she smiled, and wished he would take her into his arms and kiss her. It had been a strange week. He had been as distant from her as when she first went to work for him, and at times it didn't seem possible that she was going to be Mrs Jordan Quest. In fact she began to wonder whether she hadn't dreamt the whole thing.

'Come here.' It was almost as though he had read her mind, for his hands slid around her waist and his mouth touched hers gently. 'It's been a long week, Hannah.'

'Yes,' she whispered briefly.

'But very necessary. You've worked like a Trojan, and I appreciate it. I can leave it all now with a clear conscience. But we still have a battle on our hands at Stowley Hall. Life won't be much easier there.'

'I don't mind the hard work,' she assured him. It was the togetherness that worried her. Living with him for twenty-four hours a day, trying not to show the love that she felt for him, the love that was growing daily despite the way she had been ignored this last week. If only he loved her too! If only he wasn't marrying her for convenience's sake.

When she found herself crushed against his hard chest she felt sudden fear that he might feel her deranged heartbeats, and she struggled to free herself. But, when her head lifted, his smouldering dark eyes observed the trembling of her lips and the faint colour staining her cheeks, and with a pleased smile he claimed her mouth again, ignoring her attempts to reject him.

The kiss lasted no more than a few seconds, but in that time the raw heat of his body fused them together; Hannah felt as though she was being consumed by the intensity of emotion that swept through her. And, although she wanted to renew her struggles to escape, her limbs would not obey her command. She had become captive to his kiss.

But it was the very tonic she needed. She shopped on Saturday with a much lighter heart, Yvonne accompanying her, Yvonne advising and eventually choosing the stunning outfit for her marriage to Jordan.

Her neighbour was full of enthusiasm over the wedding. 'I only wish I could meet someone like Jordan—handsome and rich and generous. You've definitely fallen on your feet. I'm certainly going to miss you, Hannah, Danny too, but it will be good for him out in the country.'

On Sunday morning Hannah felt almost as nervous as if today were her wedding day. She had thought hard about what she ought to wear, feeling sure that none of her homemade dresses would be suitable, and in the end had bought a crêpe de Chine suit with what was left of the money from Jordan.

She looked at herself now in the mirror. The dress had a scooped neckline and a softly flowing skirt, and when she slipped on the hip-length blouson jacket she looked totally unlike her normal self. In a subtle black flower pattern on white, it was far dressier than anything else she possessed. It made her appear taller and more elegant, and at the last minute Hannah wondered whether she had overdone it.

But it was too late to change. Jordan was already at the door, Daniel running to let him in. Her heart gave its now customary surge and she smiled faintly and self-consciously as he looked at her. His appraisal was swift yet thorough, and the warmth in his eyes set her adrenalin flowing. 'You look beautiful, Hannah,' he told her. 'You'll knock my mother for six.'

'You don't think this is too dressy?' she asked, nervously pulling at the hemline of the jacket.

'Heavens, no, it's perfect. Mother will love you. Is the outfit new?'

She nodded. 'I hope you don't mind—there was some money left after I'd bought our—er—wedding clothes, and as I had nothing else really suitable I——'

'Hannah, stop!' Jordan took her fidgeting hands into his. 'That money was yours to do with as you liked, and I absolutely approve. Once we're married I'll open you a bank account and you can buy whatever clothes you need. It's time you had money to spend on yourself. I want my wife to look good, to turn heads wherever we go. I want every other man to be jealous of me.'

Hannah was not sure she could live up to that, indeed whether she wanted to. Although she was pleased with her appearance today, and it did give her confidence a boost to see herself looking so smart, she had never considered herself a very glamorous person. She was fortunate that her naturally wavy hair always looked good, even when she cut it herself; and she had never lost her figure even after she'd had Daniel. But as for anything else—well, she had never really thought too much about it.

'Shall we go?' Jordan asked with a smile, still holding her hands, still looking into her beautiful cornflower-blue eyes, still setting her pulses racing.

She nodded, and Daniel, who had been watching and waiting, dashed across to the door and opened it.

Hannah grew more and more uneasy with every minute that passed. 'What are your parents like?' she asked. 'Do you look like either of them? Are you sure they'll like me? I really don't think this is a very good idea.'

'Hannah, stop fretting! You make it sound like an ordeal. I assure you they're very normal, and my mother—well, how can she help but like you?'

There was something in his tone that made Hannah look at him sharply. He kept saying his mother would like her, but he never mentioned his father. Was his mother a very difficult person? Was it her approval he was anxious to obtain? Oh, dear, she felt sick.

'And I do actually take after my father,' he added. 'We're very much alike, in temperament as well as looks. Quick, Daniel, look, there's a Shetland pony.' They never returned to the conversation.

The cottage was well back off the road, surrounded by well-tended gardens which were a riot of colour at this time of year; a single-storeyed, brick-built building, with shining windowpanes, and roses and honeysuckle climbing everywhere. Hannah liked it on sight, but her feet dragged as she followed Jordan down the path.

Both his parents came to the door to meet them, Mr Quest Senior grey-haired and distinguished-looking, his handshake firm, his eyes friendly, Mrs Quest taller than Hannah had imagined, a dominating, beautiful woman with perfectly coiffured white hair, and a carefully veiled expression on her face. 'So you're Jordan's—fiancée?' she said, when they were inside, her slight pause indicating that she did not approve. 'Mmm, no ring, I see?' She completely ignored Daniel.

'Mother——' started Jordan.

His mother gave him a chilling glance that matched any he had given Hannah, and she saw where he had got his arrogance from. 'I believe it's all been rather sudden,' went on Mrs Quest, her finely plucked brows arched. 'I don't approve of that. I think people need time to get to know one another. Marry in haste, repent at leisure, isn't that what they say?'

Hannah glanced in horror at Jordan, an icy chill chasing down her spine, Daniel's hand clutched tightly in hers. She wished she had never agreed to come.

'Is there any reason for this hasty marriage?' Mrs Quest asked her son coldly. 'And why have you left it until the last minute to bring—*Mrs* Carpenter to meet us?' She made it very clear that the fact that Hannah had been married before was another black mark against her.

Jordan's voice matched hers for coldness. 'I thought I was doing you a courtesy, Mother, but obviously I was wrong. Don't bother to come to the wedding tomorrow, because you won't be welcome. Come, Hannah, Daniel, let's go. I'm sorry I've subjected you to this horrendous display of bad manners.'

CHAPTER EIGHT

HANNAH allowed Jordan to usher her towards the door.
She had never felt so embarrassed in her life. What a
dreadful woman his mother was! If she had known
something like this was going to happen she would never
have agreed to visit them.

'Jordan, wait!' Mrs Quest's voice had lost some of its
imperiousness. It was much quieter now and carefully
controlled.

Hannah felt him go rigid at her side, his hand tightening on her arm.

'I spoke out of turn—I—I'm sorry. But you know how
fond I am of Riva. I always wanted you to marry her,
I always thought you would. I—what happened?'

'Nothing happened,' Jordan told her coldly. 'Riva and
I are still friends—and that's all we've ever been, you
should know that. I'm marrying Hannah, and if you
can't accept her then there's no point in prolonging our
visit.'

Mrs Quest swallowed hard, visibly fighting an inner
battle, presumably realising that if she opposed this
marriage she would lose her son; perhaps for ever. 'In
that case,' her thin lips compressed, 'I'll say nothing
more.'

Jordan inclined his head, but remained tense, and it
was left to his father to step into the breach and offer
them all a glass of sherry.

It was still a very difficult day, and Hannah was glad
when Jordan suggested they leave. His mother had done

her best to make amends, but it was still clear she favoured the blonde girl, and it became obvious to Hannah during the course of the conversation that Riva had played a much larger part in Jordan's life than she had suspected.

For Jordan's sake she was civil to the older woman, pleasant even, but inside she was as cold as ice, and even in his car on their way back home she sat stiff and rigid, her hands clasped tightly in her lap.

Daniel had been as good as gold. Jordan's father had taken him out into the garden and Hannah had seen them laughing and talking together. With Mrs Quest, though, he was carefully polite, speaking only when spoken to, and Hannah knew he was afraid of her.

'I'm sorry I put you through that,' said Jordan, once they were in his car. 'My mother has always held the notion that I should marry Riva.'

'Perhaps you should,' she whispered. 'I obviously wasn't in favour.'

'It's not my mother you're marrying,' he growled. 'Don't worry about her, she'll come round.'

'But why should she want you to marry Riva if you don't love her?' Hannah insisted, forgetting for a moment that he did not love her either.

Jordan grimaced. 'My mother didn't marry for love either; she married my father for his money. I've had girls after me for that reason too,' he added bitterly.

'Is that why you scorn love so much? You think no one holds it in good esteem?'

'From my experience not many people do,' he replied cynically.

'I'd never marry a man for his money,' came her firm response.

He glanced at her and gave a wry smile. 'No, I don't think you would, Hannah. You're too straight and too honest. There aren't many girls like you. Roger was a lucky man.'

She wished she could tell him that she loved him.

When he dropped her off at the flat and she trudged up the stairs with Daniel she could not believe that tomorrow was going to be her wedding day. Apart from feeling drained after meeting his parents she felt scared, experiencing none of the excitement and happiness that had gone with her marriage to Roger. But this wasn't a normal wedding, she must not forget that, though she could not help wondering why Jordan had chosen her instead of Riva. It didn't make any sense when he was so fond of the other girl.

He obviously viewed them both differently. Riva was good for one thing, she another. She had the intelligence and aptitude to help him with his work, Riva was the proverbial dizzy blonde that a lot of men seemed to prefer but never married, and it was clear to Hannah, no matter what he said, that Riva would continue to be his mistress. The thought hurt more than she expected.

Hannah wore a cream suit and a tiny hat with a veil, and had never looked more beautiful—or so her mother said. Her parents had arrived late the night before and stayed in a small hotel, turning up at Hannah's flat in time for her mother to help her get ready.

'I'm so happy for you, Hannah,' said her mother. 'I despaired that you'd ever find yourself another man. It's a pity you didn't bring Jordan up to meet us, but if you love him, then I'm sure we will.'

Hannah could not help comparing her reaction to Mrs Quest's and gave a tiny inward smile. 'I do love him, Mummy, and so does Daniel.'

The marriage ceremony was brief, Hannah nervous and feeling sick, Jordan handsome and smiling in silver-grey. He played the part perfectly. No one attending could guess that he did not love her. It even shone out of his eyes, though how he managed that Hannah did not know. Nevertheless it was the boost she needed to get her through the day.

The small reception was held in his house on Hunter's Hill. Their respective parents, Yvonne, Drew and Daniel, were the only people present, and Daniel looked very grown-up in his first long-trousered suit. Hannah felt very proud of him.

'Jordan's perfect,' said her mother when they managed to get a moment alone. 'He's everything I could ever have wished for you. He'll look after you and Daniel, I know he will. I'm happy now.'

Hannah had been a little apprehensive about Mrs Quest, but she behaved perfectly as well, even though her congratulations were not quite as warm as her own mother's. 'You must feel free to come and visit us whenever you like,' she said, smiling insincerely. 'Tell me, where are you going for your honeymoon?'

Hannah felt a moment's panic and turned to Jordan. He had surprised her by rarely leaving her side, and how thankful she was now.

'We haven't time for a honeymoon, Mother,' he said smoothly. 'There's a lot of work to be done at Stowley Hall. We might manage one later in the year.'

His mother frowned and looked as though she was about to say something else, but Jordan took Hannah's arm and moved her swiftly away. 'I think we ought to go now,' he muttered.

She nodded, glad to be leaving this mockery of a wedding, but jittery with nerves about being alone at

Stowley Hall with Jordan. Her only salvation was Daniel. He was looking forward to moving and thought the whole affair extremely exciting.

It was a tension-filled journey, every one of Hannah's senses attuned to Jordan, unable to see what the future held, hoping only that she would not be too unhappy.

Her first impression of Stowley Hall was one of awe. She had thought Jordan's house on Hunter's Hill was grand, but it was nothing compared to this. It was a three-storeyed moated manor dating back, he told her, to the sixteenth century. It was built of stone and brick with a partly castellated roof, and Daniel's mouth fell open as he looked at it. 'Wow! Is that where we're going to live?' he demanded.

After turning off the road through a pair of wrought-iron gates with lanterns on either side they had followed a long drive which passed through dense woodland before crossing a balustraded stone bridge over the moat, ending in a sweep of gravel in front of the house.

Even though Jordan's aunt had not lived here for almost two years the windows still sparkled and there was no air of neglect, which somewhat surprised Hannah, and she said as much to Jordan.

He grinned. 'Mrs Savill, Aunt Kate's housekeeper, is a whirlwind on two feet. She has amazing energy for a woman her age. You won't find a speck of dust anywhere, even though she's lived here alone since my aunt was taken into hospital. She doted on her and kept it in readiness for her return.'

Hannah had been unaware that there was a housekeeper, but it was a relief—in more ways than one!

Arched, studded oak doors led into the porch, and the main hall beyond must have been over twenty feet long, with oak-panelled walls and a geometrically pat-

terned tiled floor. Mrs Savill came to greet them, a thin
woman with a bird-like face and quick, nervous movements. Hannah was duly introduced, and the woman
smiled warmly. 'It's good to have young people in the
house again. Is this your son? It's been many a year
since there were children running around. It'll be quite
like old times. Your trunks arrived a short time ago,
Mrs—er—Quest, and I've had them put upstairs. Supper
will be ready at seven. Is there anything else you want?'

'Not for now, thank you,' answered Jordan, and when
she had gone he said to Hannah, 'Would you like to
have a look around, or freshen up first?'

'I'll look around,' said Hannah, wanting to see all of
this wonderful place.

'Can I go outside?' asked Daniel.

'So long as you don't dirty your new suit,' she agreed.

As they wandered from room to room Hannah got
the impression of immense wealth and a house far too
big for any one single person to live in. It was at the
very least a family home, one where entertaining took
place on a large scale. The dining-room table seated
twelve people comfortably, there was also a sitting-room
and drawing-room, as well as a library and billiard-room
where Daniel would be in his element—if he were allowed to use it! Hannah could not imagine what Aunt
Kate had done with a billiard-table.

Leading from a hall at the rear of the house was the
kitchen and breakfast-room, a utility- and ironing-room,
a gun-room, a boot-room, a cloakroom. And upstairs
was even more impressive still, with nine bedrooms on
the first floor, six of them with en-suite bathrooms. It
was all too much for Hannah to take in.

Her suitcases were piled neatly in the centre of one of
the rooms, a large room with a draped four-poster bed
and tall windows with cream and rose curtains to match.

Jordan paused only briefly before leading her up another staircase to the second floor, where there were yet a further nine bedrooms. 'These were the staff quarters when the house was built,' he told her.

Hannah was overawed. 'It's too large,' she said, 'for you, or Drew, or anyone. It ought to be turned into a country hotel or a conference centre or something.'

He frowned harshly. 'Not you as well? My aunt has been approached many times by would-be developers, but she flatly refused to let it go out of the family, and I agree with her. The next thing, tenants would be turned out of their cottages and the whole estate would be one big commercial development. It would be disastrous. Some of the tenants have lived here all their lives; it's not fair that they should be disrupted. My brother doesn't agree with it, of course, that's why Aunt Kate put into her will the stipulation that he couldn't sell.'

'But the maintenance, the upkeep—it's ridiculous!' she protested. 'What did she expect Drew to do with it?'

Jordan smiled. 'Get married and raise a large family, I imagine. Run the estate as it's been run for generations. He would in effect be a gentleman farmer. Some of the land is let for sheep and cattle grazing, crops are grown. There are paddocks, a three-mile gallop, and an excellent shoot. Stop worrying your pretty head about such things. Come, let's take a look at the cellars.'

'I can't understand why she left it to Drew and not to you,' Hannah said with a frown. 'Surely you're the obvious one to take over?'

'But I have my own business, Drew has nothing. She talked it over with me, I knew exactly what was in her will.'

'Didn't she leave you anything?' she asked.

He smiled. 'Some priceless paintings to add to my collection. Don't worry, she treated us both equally.'

Hannah was not prepared for the extent and size of the cellars, carefully converted to form a small dance hall, a discotheque, bars, and well-stocked wine cellars. 'Your aunt entertained a lot?' she asked in disbelief.

'In her younger days, yes. She not only invited her own tenants, but villagers as well. She was a well liked and respected woman.'

'I'm beginning to see that.'

'It was a pity she never married,' Jordan went on. 'Her fiancé was killed in the First World War, but she never stopped loving him and never wanted any other man. It made her lonely in her old age, though. She discovered you can't live on memories for ever. You'd be as well to remember that, Hannah.'

She looked at him sharply. 'I understand how she felt.'

'And you'll never love any other man either,' he grunted impatiently. 'Is that what you're saying? It's a pity you never met my aunt, you'd have a lot in common. But you're mine now, Hannah, don't ever forget that.' He was standing behind her, and there was a determined toughness to his voice as he slid his hands about her waist and pulled her roughly against the rock-hardness of his body.

It was quiet here in the cellars, cool but not cold, an atmosphere totally different from anywhere else, a place where the strain of the day could be forgotten. Hannah felt her senses surge, and she made no protest when his mouth sought the soft skin behind her ears, allowing herself instead the drugging pleasure of his caress.

Jordan created different and exciting feelings, feelings never experienced with Roger, even though there had been nothing wrong with their sex life—or so she had thought! She had been completely satisfied, had never realised that there was anything missing—until now! It was a startling discovery.

Could Jordan offer her something Roger never had? A peak of perfection not dreamt of? The intensity of emotion that raged in her each time he kissed her far exceeded anything she had previously encountered. She wanted to fight it, to resist it, knowing it was still far too soon to give herself like this to another man. But she did not struggle when he turned her in his arms, when he kissed her eyelids, the tip of her nose, the corners of her mouth; softly, oh, so softly, until she felt her insides begin to melt. Her head fell back as his mouth moved to her throat and neck, and fire ran like quick-silver through her veins.

His kisses changed gradually from gentle pleasure to urgent need, and still Hannah did not stop him. He murmured her name against her mouth, deep, emotional hunger in his voice. He moved his hand to cup her breast, feeling the hardness of her nipple, her arousal all too evident. The buttons on her new silk blouse came easily undone.

'Jordan, I think...'

But there was no stopping him. Her breasts were eased out of their cream lace bra, supported instead by his hands, a thumb stroking, fingers squeezing. Hannah felt mindless with pleasure, but she had to stop him. It was imperative. Before she knew it they would end up in bed and he would be using her body to gratify his own needs. She did not want that. She wanted him to take her only in love. 'Jordan, please...' she began.

'Hannah, don't stop me now, don't fight me,' he groaned.

'But I'm not ready for anything like this yet,' she protested throatily.

His breath came out in a savage hiss. 'So you keep telling me, so you keep telling yourself, but it's not true. Your time of mourning has come to an end. You're my wife now, and I expect—— '

'Jordan, you promised!' Her eyes were luminous and wide and faintly apprehensive.

'I know what I promised, but I didn't realise how hard it would be,' he snarled. 'Hell, Hannah, you're my wife, and I want you. And you want me too, so don't try to deny it!' Flames of anger glittered in his eyes.

Hannah had known his patience would not last long, but she had never suspected he would want to consummate their marriage within a few hours. 'I can't give myself without love,' she whispered miserably, at the same time knowing his love would never be forthcoming.

'Love!' he jeered, thrusting her away from him. 'What is this word "love" that you keep bandying around? What is this stupid romantic notion? It means nothing. All marriage needs is mutual respect, a chemical attraction, and compatibility, and I think we have all three. I don't see what your problem is. No, that's wrong.' He pushed his face up to hers. 'I do know your problem: it's Roger. But, hell, Hannah, I refuse to have him come between us. I respect your affection for him, but he's a part of your past, I'm your present and your future, and I need you.'

He *needed* her! That was it in a nutshell. He needed her, but he didn't love her. Hannah swallowed her disappointment and turned away from him, rubbing her arms. 'It's cold down here, let's go back up.'

'Yes, let's go,' he sneered, 'let's run away. But you can't hold me at arm's length for ever. Don't for a moment think that.'

At the top of the stairs they parted company, Hannah going outside, ostensibly to look for Daniel, in truth needing to get away from Jordan for a few minutes. She felt he was suffocating her, he wasn't giving her time to come to terms with the fact that she was no longer a single woman; he wanted more from her than she was prepared to give.

Daniel was nowhere in sight, but Hannah wasn't unduly worried. The estate was vast; he was probably having the time of his life. She stood a moment surveying the neatly clipped lawns and the moat surrounding the Hall. The still water reflected clearly trees and bushes on the opposite side, and beyond were endless fields where cattle grazed. It was a heavenly spot, so peaceful, so beautiful. She did not want to go back inside. She did not want to face further torment.

But eventually she turned and made her way upstairs. She would shower and change and put away their clothes and Daniel's toys. With a bit of luck she could make the job last until supper.

To her amazement Jordan was in her room. He had changed out of his suit and wore a beige open-necked shirt with toning trousers. Her suitcases were open, clothes piled on the bed, some of them already put away in wardrobes and drawers. 'What are you doing?' she gasped.

His smile was one of satisfaction. 'Helping my wife.'

'To do what?' she frowned. 'This is *my* room, those are *my* clothes.' She snatched a pair of pink lacy briefs out of his hand. 'Get out! I'll do the unpacking myself, thank you very much.'

'This is *our* room,' he corrected her.

Her eyes darted from corner to corner, from wardrobe to wardrobe, and saw what she should have seen before—his suits and shirts hanging neatly, shoes in military straight lines. She looked back at him furiously. 'I won't share with you—it's out of the question. There are plenty of bedrooms, so why shouldn't I have my own?'

'Because you're my wife,' he answered, his calm tone belying the flicker of anger in his eyes.

'In name only,' she retorted.

'Mrs Savill isn't always the soul of discretion. I won't be made a laughing-stock, Hannah. We're sleeping together whether you like it or not!'

Hannah turned away. She felt cheated. None of the promises he had made were being kept. 'Which is Daniel's room?' she asked, her voice thick with emotion.

'Next door.'

At least that was something. She wandered through and looked at the room. It was three times as large as the one Daniel had just left. He'd love it—unlike her, he would be in his element. It had been freshly decorated in strong, bold colours, and there was even a table in one corner to hold his train-set.

'Do you approve?' Jordan spoke softly over her shoulder.

She nodded, not turning, not looking at him, but feeling the hairs prickle on the back of her neck. It was going to be difficult not responding to him, not showing how deeply he affected her—and in bed it would be even worse. He would not leave her alone, she felt sure. He would nag at her senses until in the end she gave in. It had most probably been his plan all along.

'Shall I help you put his things away?' he asked.

'No,' she whispered. 'I'd like to be left alone—if you don't mind?'

His hands touched her and turned her to him, and he saw the glint of tears in her eyes. 'Does it upset you so much, the thought of sleeping with me?' he asked huskily.

Hannah swallowed an aching lump in her throat. 'It's not what you led me to believe.'

'But you do realise how difficult it would be for us if we had separate rooms?' His thumbs gently stroked away her tears, his hands warm and firm on her cheeks.

Hannah nodded.

'It will be all right,' he assured her. 'I won't make excessive demands.'

That wasn't what worried her, it was her own feelings that were the problem, heightened beyond belief even now. How would she be able to control them? And yet control them she must. It went against every one of her principles to let Jordan use her body in lust and not love.

It was over an hour before Daniel appeared in the bedroom doorway, shamefaced and dirtier than she had ever seen him, his new suit crumpled and soiled though fortunately not torn. 'I'm sorry, Mummy,' he whispered.

She could not scold him. The upheaval was as unsettling for him as it was for her. 'It's all right,' she told him. 'Come on, let's get you bathed and changed.'

'I met some boys and we played football,' he told her.

'That's good, darling, but next time remember to come and put your old clothes on first.'

'I will, Mummy. What does that lady do downstairs? She gave me an apple. I like her.'

'She's called a housekeeper, darling,' Hannah smiled, 'and she looks after the house. She does all the cleaning and cooking and washing.'

Daniel looked pleased. 'Does that mean you'll have more time to play with me?'

'I'm afraid not,' she answered sadly. 'Jordan—er—your new father has a lot of work for me to do. I'll be very busy.'

'I'm going to call him Dad,' announced Daniel proudly. 'Not Daddy, because Daddy's not here any more. Just Dad. Do you think he'll like that?'

'I'm sure he will,' answered Hannah gently, silently applauding his choice and his logic. It pleased her that the two of them got on so well.

Daniel loved his room, as she had known he would do. 'I'm going to ask Mr—Dad to set up my trains. Can I have my new friends in to play with me?' he asked, his eyes bright and eager.

'We'll have to see about that,' replied Hannah. 'How about that bath?'

The table for supper had been set in the elegant dining-room, but Hannah was horrified at the formality. China and crystal, candles and flower arrangements. Daniel sat on the edge of his seat, and it was easy to see that he was uncomfortable too.

'This is no good,' she whispered to Jordan. 'We can't eat like this—it's too much for Daniel. Why can't we use the breakfast-room and keep this for when we have visitors? It will be easier for Mrs Savill as well, because it's nearer the kitchen. Do you think it would hurt her feelings if we suggested it?'

'I'm sure it wouldn't,' he grinned. 'She's really taken to you and Daniel. Aunt Kate always ate in here, that's why she's laid it for us.'

'Alone?' asked Hannah, astonished.

'Every evening. She dressed up too.'

'She sounds like the original aristocrat!'

'Indeed, she was a grand old lady. She was my father's sister. She never got on with my mother, but unfortunately not many people do.'

'Shall we see much of your parents now we're living so close?' asked Hannah tentatively. Jordan had told her that they were only fifteen minutes' drive away.

'Knowing my mother, yes, they'll probably drop in when we least expect them, or at least she will.'

'To see how we're getting on?' asked Hannah astutely.

Jordan nodded. 'She'd love to be able to say I told you so. By the way, did I tell you how charming I thought your parents were? It's a pity they don't live closer, I'd like to get to know them better.'

Hannah felt warmed and pleased by his praise. 'Perhaps we can take Daniel up there for a holiday once we've done most of the hard work here?'

'Perhaps,' he said. 'Or perhaps we could leave him with your parents and fly ourselves out to some tropical island for a belated honeymoon? You deserve a long, lazy, pleasure-filled holiday, Hannah.'

The mental picture conjured up in Hannah's mind of her and Jordan sunbathing on a white-hot beach, making love beneath a tropical midnight sky, brought warm colour flooding to her cheeks.

'I didn't intend to embarrass you,' he said, misconstruing her discomfort. 'But tell me, when was the last time you had a holiday?'

Hannah shrugged. 'Not a proper one since Daniel was born. We've been up to Scotland a few times, but there was never enough money for anything else once I was no longer working.'

'All the more reason why you should let me take you away,' he said softly. 'But that's all in the future, there's far too much work to be done here first.' His tone changed, became brisk and businesslike. 'When we've finished our meal and put Daniel to bed we'll take a walk around the estate—you need to familiarise yourself with it. Tomorrow we'll start work.'

In all there were six semi-detached cottages and one farmhouse on the estate. Five of the cottages were tenanted, one was vacant. All were in need of repair, and the vacant one was in the worst state of all.

I could live here, thought Hannah. It wouldn't take much to knock it into shape. I needn't have married Jordan. I could do his work from here, and I'd be happier.

'Is something wrong?' he asked, when she stood looking at the white-painted building for so long.

'It's a bit like the cottage I lived in with Roger,' she said quietly.

Jordan drew in a deep breath. 'So even here I can't get away from him?' he rasped.

Hannah looked at him in hurt self-defence. 'I can't forget him.'

With an angry grunt he swung away from her and headed back towards the Hall. Hannah did not bother to follow. It was his own fault if he was so touchy where Roger was concerned.

She wandered further and spotted the stables and the horses in the paddock, and wondered if Daniel had seen them too. The farmer had sometimes let him ride one of his ponies, and it had been Danny's ambition to own his own horse when he grew up.

It was growing dark when she eventually made her way back to the Hall. She crept upstairs, hoping to be in bed and asleep before Jordan joined her, starting in surprise when she snapped on the light and saw him sitting in one of the coral-pink armchairs by the window.

He must have seen her come back. He had been sitting there watching and waiting, and now there was no escaping him.

'I'd better check on Daniel,' she murmured quickly, her pulses beating much too fast.

'There's no need, I've already done it.'

His eyes were on her, and what she saw there brought fresh colour to her throat and cheeks. 'I'll go and shower, then. I feel hot and sticky.'

'Don't be long,' he warned.

She stood beneath the cooling jets with closed eyes and a body that was alien to her. Not even when she married Roger and was still a virgin had she felt like this. Excited, extremely excited, but afraid too; sexually aroused but not ready to give herself, hungry for love but knowing she must hold back. Jordan was not Roger. Jordan did not love her. Jordan enjoyed sex for the sake of sex. She could not go through with it. She ought not to have married him.

'Hannah!' His harsh voice penetrated her thoughts, but she was not prepared for the shower door to slide sharply open and Jordan's naked body to ease in beside her. 'If you're going to stay in here all night then I might as well join you,' he growled.

The feel of his wet skin brushing against her own added further floods of sensation. And when he began to soap her, to move his hands slowly and sensually and possessively over her trembling body, feeling each intimate curve, she knew that the last of her defences were in danger of crumbling.

It was the first time she had taken a shower with a man, and it felt faintly indecent, but stimulating and thrilling at the same time. In fact, it was the most erotic thing that had ever happened to her, and she had to fight the urge to touch him in a similar manner.

'Oh, Hannah,' he muttered, 'you're even more beautiful than I dreamt!' His eyes were dark with desire, intent on her, willing her to respond, willing her to throw off the iron bonds that still shackled her. 'So beautiful, so lovely.' His fingers lightly stroked her heated cheeks and touched her parted, quivering lips. 'This is our wedding night, a night for making love.' His eyes darkened with an emotion deeper than anything she had seen before. 'And tonight I intend to make you mine.'

She turned off the shower, but it was several long seconds before she summoned the nerve to step out and wrap herself in a large, fluffy towel. It had been an ordeal to her hard not to think, but tonight, into the bedroom but it would be madness he would have to draw in case of Jordan, and he would no doubt that only...

CHAPTER NINE

JORDAN'S declaration that he was going to make love to her made Hannah equally determined not to let him. He wanted her for all the wrong reasons. He was using her emotions, he was using the power of his own body, and all it added up to was sex—pure, unadulterated sex. And that wasn't what marriage was about.

When she edged away from him a puzzled frown narrowed his eyes. 'Hannah?' he queried.

'I'm sorry,' she whispered huskily. 'I don't want you to—to touch me, I don't want you to——'

Disbelief flared. 'Liar! Even if you won't admit it your body tells me otherwise. Would you like me to prove it?'

She shook her head and flattened herself even further back against the side of the shower cubicle. Her hair hung in dripping wet tendrils around her face, and with the heat and the steam bringing a rose bloom to her cheeks she had no idea how beautiful and vulnerable she looked.

'Hannah!' It was a deep, throaty groan, and he moved towards her, but when she put out her hands to ward him off anger hissed through his teeth. 'If that's the game you want to play,' he rasped, fury turning his eyes to stone, 'then let's see which one of us is sorry first!'

He snapped open the cubicle door and slammed it back again, and Hannah felt tears sting her eyes. It had been hard denying him, but this was no ordinary marriage, and she was not going to let him pretend it was.

She turned off the shower, but it was several long seconds before she summoned the nerve to step out and wrap herself in a large, fluffy towel. It had been an omission on her part not to bring her nightie into the bathroom, for it now meant that she would have to dress in front of Jordan, and he would no doubt insolently watch and enjoy every minute.

For the second time she was wrong in her assumption. Jordan was nowhere in sight. Glad of the reprieve, Hannah quickly towelled herself dry, pulled on her nightdress, brushed her hair, and jumped into bed. She felt quite breathless by the time she had finished and lay beneath the pink silken canopy, panting and tense, waiting for him to come back into the room.

She waited a long time, so long in fact that her lids grew heavy and she fell asleep. She woke again a few hours later to find the bed beside her still empty, but when she opened her eyes the next time the room was bathed in early morning sunlight and Jordan was standing, fully dressed, in front of the window. In those few seconds before he realised she was awake she glanced hungrily at him, wondering if she had been a fool to deny herself the pleasure he could undoubtedly give her. In the shower last night he had awoken senses and feelings that she had never experienced in all the years she had been married to Roger.

Jordan's dark, rugged good looks were in sharp relief, the planes of his face still taut with inner anger, his shirt and trousers doing nothing to hide the muscular hardness of his body. Hannah felt the muscles bunch in her stomach and for a fleeting second wished her principles weren't so strong.

Trying to ignore the ache, she turned her head away—then saw a depression in the other pillow! Her breath caught. She did not want to believe that he had slept with her, but here was indisputable proof.

'Good, you're awake.' His voice mocked from the other side of the room. 'You'd better get down to breakfast before it goes cold.'

'What time is it?' she frowned, relieved he had made no mention of last night.

'Eight o'clock.'

Eight o'clock and Daniel wasn't up! 'Why didn't you wake me?' she cried, throwing back the sheets and springing out of bed. 'Danny will be late for the first day at his new school!' Only belatedly did she realise that she was wearing a near-diaphanous nightgown.

But she could have been wearing nothing for all the notice Jordan took. His voice was starkly cold as he said, 'Daniel's ready. I saw to him myself. He's waiting for you in the breakfast-room.'

'You needn't have done that,' she said sharply, 'he's my responsibility.'

'I don't see it in quite that light.' His eyes blazed into hers. 'As you are now my wife, he is my son.'

'Not in the eyes of the law, Jordan. He's still a Carpenter!' she thrust back furiously.

'For the moment,' he answered, his tone icy cold. 'I intend to see about getting that changed. And I'm afraid Daniel doesn't share your views. He's actively welcomed me into his life. It was me he woke this morning, me he asked to help him get ready for school. Does that suggest he doesn't see me as his new father? He actually called me Dad!' There was a pleased and happy note to his voice as he spoke.

Hannah wasn't surprised that Daniel had changed his allegiance so quickly, but she did not like it, and the thought of him coming into their room and seeing her

in bed with Jordan made her feel distinctly uncomfortable; though no more so, she supposed, than if he
had found her sleeping alone. There would certainly have
been questions asked then.

'I'll get washed straight away,' she muttered, ignoring
his question, heading for the bathroom and closing the
door firmly between them.

But the next second it was pushed savagely open. 'I
want no closed doors between us, Hannah. You're my
wife, and don't you forget it. I'll see you downstairs.'

The relief when he had gone was enormous, and
Hannah stood a moment at the wash-basin steadying
herself, wondering if this was how it was going to be.
Would he lose no opportunity to remind her that they
were husband and wife and expect her to behave ac-
cordingly? Couldn't he accept the fact that this was a
marriage with a difference, that she had as much right
to privacy as if they weren't married at all?

When she walked into the breakfast-room Jordan and
Daniel were deep in urgent conversation, and although
it should have done her heart good to see them getting
on so well Hannah felt herself resenting their closeness.

'Mummy, Mummy,' said Daniel, sliding off his chair
and running across the room to give her a hug, 'guess
what Dad's promised me?' The name slipped easily off
his tongue.

'I don't know, what has he promised you?' she asked.

'A pony,' he announced grandly. 'A pony of my very
own!'

'That's lovely, darling,' she said, at the same time
glaring at Jordan over the top of her son's head. This
really was taking things too far! It amounted to buying
her son's affection. Daniel would begin to think that

whatever he asked for he could have—and he had never been brought up that way.

Hannah did her best to join in the conversation over the breakfast table, but all in all it was Daniel and Jordan who did most of the talking, and Jordan who offered to take Daniel to school, which, much to her annoyance, he accepted with alacrity.

The school was actually only a few minutes' walk away from the estate, but even so Daniel somehow persuaded Jordan to take him in his Ferrari. Hannah knew it was to impress the other children, and the thought that he was getting conscious of the power of money at the tender age of nine angered her even further.

But for the moment she kept her thoughts to herself, kissing Daniel goodbye, telling him to be good, and feeling proud of him in his brand-new grey and red uniform. He had not worn a uniform at his other school—now he looked suddenly so much more grown-up, and she felt a lump of maternal pride in her throat. She wanted to go with them, but pride forbade her from asking. Daniel was clearly happy alone with Jordan. So many responsibilities were being taken from her, yet instead of feeling happy and relieved she felt miserable, and wished, not for the first time, that she had not let Jordan persuade her to marry him.

As there was nothing to do while waiting for Jordan to come back Hannah took a stroll in the grounds. It was alien to her not to have to wash the dishes and make the beds, but she sensed that if she dared to offer any help Mrs Savill would be up in arms. She had cooked them an excellent breakfast of bacon, sausages and egg, and Daniel had tucked in heartily. It was more than he was ever used to eating in the morning, but to Hannah's surprise he had managed every bit.

Jordan was away no more than the few minutes she had expected and he joined her by the side of the moat. 'You're spoiling Daniel,' she accused as he walked up to her.

'Because I took him to school in the car?' Thick brows rose questioningly.

'That as well,' she snapped. 'He'll expect it every day; but what's bothering me most is you offering to buy him a pony. He's not used to such expensive gifts. Before you know it it will be ask and have, and I won't allow that.'

'Isn't a pony every kid's dream?' Jordan asked.

'A dream, yes, but not always reality.'

'Only when parents can't afford it.'

Hannah shook her head impatiently. 'It always boils down to money, doesn't it? People with money never seem to realise what harm it does. I'm not going to ask you to go back on your word, but please don't make any more such extravagant gestures. Shall we go in and start work?'

'I don't agree with your line of reasoning,' he said shortly, 'but yes, we'd better make a start. I'll save my argument for another occasion.'

The estate office was next door to the library. It was not a very big room, looking as though a second desk had been brought in to accommodate them both, and Hannah dreaded the thought of working in such close proximity for hours on end.

There were ledgers and sheets of paper all over the place. It was the untidiest office Hannah had ever seen. She looked at it in dismay. 'It will take ages just to get this lot sorted out!'

'Precisely,' he said grimly. 'I don't think anything has been done properly since my aunt was taken into hospital.'

They worked in surprising harmony for the rest of the morning, stopping only when Mrs Savill brought them coffee at eleven and sandwiches for their lunch at one. 'I hope you don't mind,' Jordan said. 'I thought a cooked lunch would take up too much time.'

Hannah shrugged. 'You're the boss.'

His watchful eyes narrowed. 'I prefer to think we're a team.'

'Because I'm your wife?' she asked crisply.

'Because you're my wife,' he agreed. 'Though I'm beginning to have my doubts whether I've made the right decision.'

'I certainly think you haven't,' said Hannah before she could stop herself. 'I can't see us ever living together as a husband and wife should.'

'Why is that?' he asked coldly. 'And don't try to put the blame on me.'

'I wouldn't dream of it,' she answered, her tone sharp. 'The trouble is, we're not compatible. I married you for all the wrong reasons.'

'Like security?'

She nodded.

'Like a father for your son?'

Again she inclined her head.

'But we both knew these things before you agreed,' he rasped. 'What else is wrong that you're not telling me?'

Love was wrong, or rather the lack of it—on his part, Hannah thought bitterly. 'It's all wrong.'

'You think I'm going to spoil Daniel, is that it?'

'Partly,' she agreed.

'And the other part, it wouldn't have anything to do with Roger, by any chance?' Jordan's eyes narrowed on her face. 'Is that why you shrank away from me in the shower? You don't want me to touch you, you said. Is it so abhorrent, the thought of another man in his place? Is that what all this is about, Hannah?'

She nodded. It was easier to lie than tell him the truth.

'I'll make you feel differently!' he snarled, and for one moment Hannah thought he was going to pull her into his arms there and then. 'But I'll give you time to get used to the idea of me sharing your life—and your bed!' he finished darkly. 'I'll put no pressure on you, but before I've finished I guarantee you'll be begging me to touch you, to make love to you, to share every intimate thought. You'll melt in my arms at the slightest caress, at a whisper, at a glance. We'll be lovers as no other people have been lovers before, and we'll be husband and wife in the true sense of the word.'

Never the true sense, she thought, never that. Lovers maybe. Even as Jordan spoke Hannah felt some of his threatened power shudder through her. Little did he realise how fragile her defences were against his savage sensuality.

'And now,' he said, his dark eyes still intent on her face, 'back to work.'

But everything had changed with those few words. Constantly now she felt his eyes on her, a message in their depths that could not be ignored, and it became more and more difficult for her to concentrate. She was glad when a telephone call took his attention for over half an hour, and when he had finished he was once again the brisk businessman. 'One day I've left them, that's all, and there's a problem no one can handle,' he growled. 'I'll be gone for the rest of the day, Hannah.

I'm sorry about this. When you finish sorting this lot perhaps you can send letters to each of the tenants asking them to list whatever repairs need doing.'

Hannah nodded.

'And you'll have to fetch Daniel, although I promised him I'd be there myself.'

'I'll go,' she said, controlling her sudden anger with difficulty. He was making it sound as though Daniel was his son and she was the one doing the favour.

It was such a relief when he had gone that Hannah sat for ages doing nothing, savouring only the peace of her surroundings. Stowley Hall was a beautiful house, but she would never be content here, always she would need to be on her guard.

She sat so long that it was time to fetch Daniel before she realised it. The walk down to the school helped calm her troubled mind, and she was smiling happily until Daniel came running out of the school gates with tears streaming down his cheeks. 'I don't like that school, Mummy!' he cried. 'I don't want to go again. Please don't send me there again!' But it was not until they got back to the Hall that she managed to get out of him what was wrong.

Jordan's Ferrari was the trouble. The children who had seen him arrive had immediately dubbed him a snob, had taunted him all day long and made his life a complete misery. Hannah tried to tell him that he should not take any notice, that all schools had bullies who took it out of new boys, but he wouldn't be pacified, and when Jordan came home a few hours later he poured all his troubles out to him.

'I think we need a good man-to-man talk,' said Jordan, and with a look at Hannah that said leave this to me, he took Daniel up to his room.

When he returned, alone, she said anxiously, 'How is he?'

'He's all right,' he assured her. 'It's perfectly understandable that he should be upset; he's gone through a lot, poor kid, over the last couple of years. But he's no coward. We had a good chat, and he's quite happy about going back to school.'

'Are you sure?' frowned Hannah.

'Of course. You fuss too much. He definitely has the guts to stick up for himself—so long as you don't keep mollycoddling him. I was right in that he needed a father-figure. There are obviously lots of things that you're not capable of handling.'

'Where's Danny now?' she asked coldly, resenting his implication.

'In his room, getting ready for bed. He wants you to go up, but whatever you do don't sympathise with him, or you'll undo all the good I've done. I'm going to see Jim Browne, the farmer—I'll see you when I get back.'

How dared he tell her how to treat her own son? Hannah was furious as she ran up the stairs, and she had to pause a minute outside Daniel's door to compose herself.

To give Jordan his due, Daniel was relaxed and happy again, and as she kissed him goodnight and tucked him in he said sleepily, 'I love you, Mummy, and I love Dad as well. I love him lots. We're a proper family again now.'

A proper family! She repeated his words over and over as she went back down. *A proper family!* How little Daniel knew of the true situation. But if that was how he felt then she was glad she had married Jordan. If it made her son happy then she was happy. A marriage of convenience it might be on Jordan's part, but she loved him and Daniel loved him, that was all that mattered.

When Jordan joined her in the sitting-room with its moss-green carpet and beige and rose chairs, and French windows which opened out on to a sunken garden at the back of the Hall, she had a magazine open on her lap, but her thoughts were anywhere except on the printed page.

He flopped down tiredly on to one of the deep armchairs and closed his eyes. 'Shall I make you some coffee?' Hannah asked tentatively.

'I'd prefer a whisky,' he said, jumping up again and going across to a cupboard which Hannah saw held a wide selection of drinks. 'Won't you join me?'

Hannah shook her head. 'I don't drink.'

'Then it's about time you started,' he said thickly, pouring a gin and tonic, adding ice out of a refrigerated compartment next to the drinks cupboard and handing it to her without another word. Their fingers touched, and a jolt ran through her, and as she looked up into the velvet brown of his eyes she saw that they were flecked with gold. Strange how she had not noticed before. He had thick, silky black lashes that sometimes screened his expression, but not at this moment. His eyes were making love to her, letting her know without words that he found her beautiful and desirable.

The look lasted no more than a few seconds, but it was long enough to stir Hannah's senses, and she wriggled uncomfortably on her seat. 'Danny's gone to sleep,' she said needlessly.

'Good, I'm glad he's settled, he was in quite a state.' Jordan finished pouring his own drink and sat down again, his eyes still on hers. 'Let's drink a toast, Hannah, a toast to us, to happiness and a long married life.'

How could you achieve happiness without love? she wondered. It didn't have to be a deep love. If only he would love her just a little bit, just enough to warrant her giving herself to him. If he did not love her, if he never loved her, the hungry ache in her heart would one day become unbearable. 'A toast to us,' she said faintly.

'You don't seem too sure?' A frown appeared, grooving two deep lines in his brow.

'How can I be sure under the circumstances?'

'Hannah,' his emphasis on the last syllable of her name had never been more pronounced, 'you married me for better or worse. There's no backing out. I might not believe in love, but I don't believe in divorce either. You're stuck with me now for the rest of your life.'

Hannah said nothing. What was there to say?

'Are you regretting it already—after only one day?' She shook her head.

'Then I suggest you smile and at least pretend to be happy. You've got me now instead of Roger, so accept it and make the most of things.' There was a caustic bite to his tone and the softness had gone out of his eyes.

'I'll try,' she murmured, not wishing to arouse his temper by saying it was impossible.

'You'd better,' he growled, taking a long swallow of his whisky.

Hannah drank her gin also, but too quickly, and she choked as it went down the wrong way. Tears came to her eyes and she saw Jordan in a blur as he rose to pat her back.

'There's no need,' she demurred.

'Of course, I'd forgotten you don't like me touching you,' he grated. 'I think maybe I'll take my drink through to the office and go through some more papers. Did you do those letters?'

Hannah shook her head. 'I didn't have time.'

'So what the hell were you doing while I was away?'

'I went to fetch Daniel, and then——'

'You decided not to go back to work?' Jordan cut in accusingly. 'You decided to smother him with love and make the whole situation worse.'

'I did not!' protested Hannah.

He snorted impatiently. 'I imagine I've married you just in time to stop him becoming a spoilt mother's boy who can't stick up for himself.'

'If it hadn't been for your stupid Ferrari none of this would have happened,' she riposted.

'I don't agree,' he told her smoothly. 'Most boys get taunted. It's a matter of giving as good as you get. All Daniel needed was a boost to his self-confidence. I think our talk helped. I'm sure he won't allow them to upset him again.'

Why was it that Jordan always knew what to do? she mused. It was a pity he'd never had a son of his own— he would certainly have been a boy to be proud of. But so was Danny, she told herself. He was a little timid, a little shy, but that was all, and now with Jordan for a father he would... Her thoughts came to an abrupt halt. She was already, in her mind, letting Jordan take over.

'What are you thinking now?' he asked, seeing her change of expression.

'Nothing.'

Again his brows rose in that familiar manner when he did not believe she was speaking the truth. 'That's a psychological impossibility.'

'OK, nothing that I want to tell you,' Hannah amended.

'Because it concerns me?'

'Really, Jordan, I don't have to answer all these questions!'

He smiled then, a slow smile that softened the hard planes of his face and sent tiny lines radiating out from the corners of his eyes. 'That means the answer was yes. But I won't press you—it's your privilege to think what you like.'

The moment he left the room Hannah finished her drink and went upstairs to bed. It was early, far too early, but she wanted to be asleep before Jordan came up, and she knew she would lie awake for a long time before she eventually dropped off.

She had been in bed for no more than a few minutes when he came into their room. She had been alerted by the sound of his brisk footsteps outside the door and now lay with her eyes tightly closed, pretending to be asleep.

But when she heard the rustle of a silky shirt being slid from broad shoulders, and a trouser zip being carefully lowered, her eyes shot wide. 'What are you doing?'

He smiled lazily. 'Joining my wife—what do you think? It can only mean one thing when you come to bed at this hour.'

'But—but you didn't know I was here,' she spluttered, growing hot and cold alternately. He was playing some sort of cat-and-mouse game, shredding her nerves.

'I came in search of you. I was going to ask you a question about the accounts, but naturally that can wait. This is a far more pleasant way of spending the evening.' By now all he was wearing was a pair of brief black underpants.

A warm flush coloured her cheeks as she saw the way he was looking at her. It needed no guesswork to know what was in his mind. And yet he had promised! Or was this all part of the torment? Was he going to join her in bed but not touch her? Arouse her desires to fever pitch but do nothing about it? Wait for her to make the first move?

CHAPTER TEN

HANNAH watched as though hypnotised until Jordan finally stood naked before her. In the shower he had been too close for her to see his body clearly, now she saw his powerful physique for the first time, and her breath caught in her throat at the magnificence of his body. Her eyes were drawn to his very evident state of arousal, and although she wanted to turn her head away she somehow couldn't; she was caught in some sort of spell.

Jordan himself was sublimely indifferent to his nakedness, smiling softly to himself as he moved over to the bed, sliding slowly and threateningly—as far as Hannah was concerned—beneath the sheets. She did not edge away; that would have given him too much satisfaction. Instead she lay perfectly still, her hands clenched, her whole body as taut as a violin string.

For several long seconds he lay there facing her, carefully not touching, breathing quietly and evenly. Even though she kept her eyes resolutely closed she knew he was watching her, and every one of her nerve-ends tingled with awareness and anticipation.

'Do you think you can shut me out if you don't look at me?' he asked, his voice a low, sexy growl, adding another layer of disturbance to her soul.

'No,' she answered with a soft shake of her head.

'Then I suggest you open your beautiful eyes. I don't like being treated as though I'm not here.'

With difficulty Hannah complied, but her lids were so heavy she had to force them open. And when she discovered his face mere inches away from her own every muscle in her body froze.

'That's better,' he said huskily. 'Now I can see what you're thinking.'

This was what she had been afraid of. He seemed to have the uncanny knack of knowing everything that was going on in her mind.

'Don't you miss having a man in your bed? Isn't it lonely in the middle of the night? Doesn't your body ache to be possessed?'

The provocative sentences were posed slowly and one at a time, and Hannah felt a fresh flood of feelings with each taunt. 'Of course I miss Roger,' she whispered faintly, 'and yes, it is lonely, but no, I don't ache to be possessed by any man.'

Jordan's eyes narrowed faintly. 'I think you're lying— I think that even at this very moment you're aching.'

'No,' she denied painfully.

'No?' An eyebrow rose. 'You feel no response at all to me? I don't believe that, Hannah.'

'Of course I feel—something,' she stammered. 'It wouldn't be natural if I didn't.'

'But you don't want to do anything about it?' His brown eyes were fixed intently on hers, exciting further emotions, and Hannah knew she would not be able to pretend indifference much longer.

'I can't,' she whispered. 'I loved Roger too much.' She stuck to her old story. It was her only defence.

A muscle jerked fiercely in his jaw. 'So we're back to that again!' There was a rough edge to his voice now, and Hannah shivered faintly. 'It's like a well-worn

record, and I'm getting sick and tired of it. Try changing
your tune.'

Hannah said nothing, wishing herself a hundred miles
away.

'Cat got your tongue?' he taunted. 'Or is the truth
sinking in? Is your mind ticking away and any minute
now it will come up with a response?'

She swallowed hard. 'Why do you treat me like this?'
she whispered.

'Why? Why do you treat me the way you do, when I
know full well that your denial is hurting yourself as
well as me?'

How could he know that? How could he be so sure
she was hurting? Hannah closed her eyes again, and immediately opened them when firm fingers grasped her
chin.

'Don't do that to me,' he warned. 'Don't ever try to
ignore me.' His bruising grip relaxed and his touch
became a caress. Hannah closed her eyes in pleasure this
time, then quickly opened them again before he could
complain. He touched her lower lip, easing it down with
an incredibly gentle finger and stroking the moist softness
inside, his eyes on what he was doing instead of on hers.

There was total concentration on his face, though she
had no idea what thoughts were going through his mind.
He seemed to find her mouth fascinating, running
his now moistened finger around the outline of her lips,
parting them, inciting tiny flames of desire so that
without conscious thought Hannah's tongue reached out
and touched his finger, mingling, thrilling, shooting
arrows of pleasurable excitement through her quivering
body.

Every one of her pulses raced, there was an aching
lump in the base of her throat, and when his hand slid

behind her head, his face moving with painful slowness towards hers, his intention to kiss her perfectly clear, she hadn't the strength or the will to stop him.

But the kiss did not materialise, not as she had imagined. His lips brushed hers with the lightness of the stroke of an artist's paintbrush, the tip of his tongue tracing the path his finger had taken earlier, and then he withdrew.

Hannah could not believe that this was all he was going to do, and she looked at him with wide, surprised eyes.

He smiled, faintly and enigmatically. 'Is something wrong?'

'I expected more,' she breathed, then regretted her honesty.

'Expected, or wanted?' he asked with a faintly cynical smile.

'I can't believe you're so gentle, so undemanding.' Hannah frowned slightly as she spoke. 'It's not what I expect from you.'

'What did you imagine?' His hand rested on the creamy skin of her throat, his thumb stroking the soft down on her cheek, a treacherous caress that lit fires and awoke dangerous senses.

She suddenly realised that his leg now lay next to hers, moving as insidiously as his fingers, arousing, igniting, deliberately tormenting.

When she did not answer he muttered thickly, 'I'm not always this patient, but they say that if something is worth having it's worth waiting for. And do you know what, Hannah? I'm enjoying this game far more than I thought possible.'

Her lips twisted bitterly. 'I always knew it was a game to you.'

'What do you expect when you constantly hold me at arm's length?' Jordan asked wryly. 'I'm only human, I need some light relief.'

'And playing with my emotions is entertainment?'

'Your *emotions*?' he asked, thick black eyebrows raised sceptically. 'I don't think so, not if you're telling me the truth. There are no emotions involved as far as you're concerned; they're still tied to a man who's no longer here.' There was a sudden edge of savage bitterness to his tone. 'It's sex we're talking about at this moment, pure unadulterated sex. You want me and I want you—it's that simple.'

With a sudden, unexpected movement a leg and an arm were thrown over her and she was pulled against the hair-roughened hardness of his unyielding body. Hot lips scorched a trail from her cheek to her ear to her mouth. Her heartbeats quickened convulsively and the room whirled as her breathing became slow and tortured.

She wanted him so much, had dreamt of this moment so often, that she was unable to protest. The time had come when she could fight him no longer. Her trembling arms slid hungrily around him, her fingernails biting into firm, warm flesh as excitement tore through her like a hurricane in full force.

Jordan paused for a brief, questioning moment, glazed eyes meeting, desire flaring in both brown and blue, and with a deep groan of satisfaction his hot mouth sought the aching fullness of her breasts. Sensual pleasure such as she had never felt before shot through every pulsing inch of her, and although she felt a moment's misgiving because she was responding so eagerly when he did not love her, it failed to last.

'You're so beautiful,' he muttered hoarsely, 'so soft and warm and sweet. I never thought you'd let me——'

'Please, don't talk.' Hannah felt that words would ruin everything, the magical spell would be broken and her conscience would force her to stop him.

He sighed as he resumed his assault on her body, searching out with his hands and his lips and his tongue each intimate, sweetly smelling curve. Hannah moaned her pleasure, passion mounting, her hands moulding his head, holding him against her writhing body, never wanting him to let her go. All thoughts of being disloyal to Roger had fled. Her late husband had never made her feel like this, she had never felt so—so wanton, so primevally hungry for love. All she hoped was that he wouldn't arouse her to a state of complete abandon and then stop, that this wasn't a form of punishment for the way she had always rejected him.

The next time his mouth claimed hers she was shocked into responding so feverishly that it was as if a stampede had taken place in her body. Relentlessly he drew her against him until she felt every hard bone. Their lips clung, frantic hearts beating simultaneously, the room spinning around them until they became one.

'God, Hannah,' Jordan groaned savagely against her mouth, 'how I've waited for this moment! Ever since I met you I've wanted you.' His lips were warm and soft and moist, his hand firm on the small of her back, holding her pliant body resolutely against him.

He didn't have to remind her that this was his only reason for making love, she thought resentfully, but, in the grip of emotions so powerful that they hurt, she ignored his words and opened her mouth up to his again. She found it difficult to believe that he could drive her to such rapture, to such dizzy heights that she had never once found with Roger. And this was merely the start!

She pressed herself unashamedly against him, and as he muttered against her mouth his voice grew thicker and thicker until she could no longer tell what he was saying. Crazed, mindless whimperings escaped her throat as his exploration of her body became more and more urgent, until finally her own voice, strangled and unrecognisable, begged him to make love to her.

His actions, at first gentle, suddenly became those of a man who had lost control, hands and body impatient, and Hannah felt a wonderful, magical upsurge of her senses as she welcomed him into her. So long she had rejected him, so long she had warded him off, so long she had fought her own conscience, and now, sweet, fierce intimacy; an emotion charged with such power and energy that it threatened to burn her up.

She responded with wildly feverish abandonment, white-hot sensations rocketing through her, climaxing in an explosion of feeling that left no corner of her body untouched, Jordan groaning as though in pain and shuddering in violent reaction almost at the same time.

They lay quietly in each other's arms, Hannah in awe of the unexpectedly intense emotions he had been able to create in her, drifting on a plane far above mere mortals. Making love had never been like this before; her throbbing body felt warm and completely satiated— and there were still further heights waiting to be scaled! It was a sensual world Jordan had taken her into, a world of senses and feelings never imagined, a world where passion dominated and no reservations were allowed.

'No regrets, Hannah?' His voice was low and unsteady, and she felt further faint tremors shaking his body like the aftermath of an earthquake.

'None.' There was a quiver in her voice too, and she did not want to be aroused out of her state of euphoric lethargy. It felt right now here beside him; this was where she belonged, this was where she wanted to stay for ever—irrespective of the fact that he did not love her. It was sufficient that he was fond enough of her to marry her, and surely there was enough love in her heart for the two of them?

How long she lay there drifting in and out of sleep Hannah did not know, aware only that each time she awoke Jordan's hands were caressing a different part of her body. She whimpered faintly as hunger ignited within her again, and began caressing him too, letting him know how she felt with no shame at all.

He guided and encouraged, and she discovered new and exciting ways of giving and receiving pleasure, making her realise that Roger's technique had been very limited. She had never in her wildest dreams imagined that making love could be so sensual, so soul-disturbing, so entirely, entirely erotic. She felt an animal hunger that threatened to tear her apart and was matched equally by his. Her surrender was absolute.

Afterwards, tucked into the curve of Jordan's arm, she fell into a much deeper sleep. Roger came to her in her dreams. They sat and talked, and she told him about Jordan and he was pleased that she had found someone else. He had been worried, he said, about her being all alone, but now he knew that he need worry no longer. He kissed her, a tender kiss that was a goodbye and a thank-you for all the happy years, and Hannah awoke feeling more at peace with herself than she had in a long time.

When she opened her eyes she saw Jordan, fully dressed, looking down at her. She smiled sleepily and held out her hand, but he ignored it and told her sharply to get up.

She frowned, feeling some of the happiness drain out of her. 'Is something wrong?' she asked.

'Why should there be? Get showered and dressed while I see to Daniel.'

'Didn't—didn't I please you last night?' she asked faintly.

'I said get up,' he snapped.

Hannah climbed out of bed, but still hesitated. 'Jordan, I—what's wrong?'

'Nothing's wrong, except it's late. I have to go to the works again today and I promised Daniel I'd take him to school first.'

'There's no need for that,' she retorted, her tone now as sharp as his. Something had happened in his mind that he was not letting her be privy to, but she was not going to let him run her life. 'Besides, after what happened to my son yesterday I don't think it would be wise to take him in your Ferrari.'

'What happened yesterday is the very reason I'm taking him,' he countered coldly.

Hannah could see there was no point in arguing with Jordan in this frame of mind, but she wished he would tell her what was bothering him. Did he regret last night? Hadn't she satisfied him? Was he disappointed? Did she compare abysmally to Riva? Perhaps it had been a test? It was obvious he wanted nothing more to do with her.

Tears smarted at the backs of her eyes as she followed him into Daniel's room, and her unhappiness increased as she saw him gently shaking her son's arm, his expression now one of complete tenderness, proving that she alone was the butt of his anger.

Over breakfast Daniel was so busy chattering that it was not obvious she and Jordan weren't on speaking terms. 'Don't forget those letters today,' were his only words as he left the house.

Hannah sat for many minutes in the office going over the events of the night, trying to think what she might have done to upset Jordan, coming up with nothing except that she couldn't have pleased him, and deciding once again that it must have something to do with Riva's prowess as a lover.

It was a long day. She kept expecting Jordan back at any minute, and every little sound had her looking out of the window. She could not help wondering whether Riva had called into the office to see him, whether he had taken her out to lunch, whether he had... The thought galled, it stuck in her throat like a piece of dry bread.

The telephone rang a few seconds before she was due to fetch Daniel from school. Her pulses accelerated when she heard Jordan's deep voice, but her joy quickly diminished when he said crisply, 'I'm on my way, and I'll pick Daniel up.' There was no hint of warmth at all. Whatever the bone of contention between 'em, it was still there. Hannah closed her eyes wearily as she replaced the receiver. All day she had been hoping things would somehow right themselves. Now it was obvious that there was no change. It was going to be quite an evening—and goodness knew what would happen when they went to bed.

If nothing else was going the right way, at least Daniel came running in all smiles and happiness. 'No one's bothered me today, Mummy. Can I go out to play?'

She smiled and hugged him. 'Once you're changed, yes. But be back at five for your tea.' She had arranged with Mrs Savill for him to eat early.

As soon as Daniel had gone out, an apple in one hand and a ball in the other, Hannah returned to the office. She had placed the letters in a neat pile on Jordan's desk, and he sat there reading them before adding his signature with its usual flourish. 'You can deliver these by hand later,' he said coldly. 'What else have you been doing today?'

'Still tidying up, but it's all done now.' He looked tired, she thought, lines of strain on his face that had not been there yesterday, and a blank expression in his eyes that shut her out. 'Have you had a bad day? What was the problem?'

'It's no longer any of your business.' His tone was so sharp it cut into Hannah's nerves like a knife, making her wince and step back and wonder what she had done to merit this sort of treatment.

'I realise that,' she said quietly and evenly, 'but as your wife I'm interested in whatever it is that's making you look so tired.'

'Wife?' The word was shot at her like a dart from a blowpipe. 'I must have been out of my mind to even suggest marriage! But what's done is done, there's no going back. Get your notebook, I want to dictate some more letters.'

But Hannah did not move. 'I want to know what it is I've done that's made you like this. Last night we——'

'Last night makes no difference to how I feel now,' Jordan cut in coldly and contemptuously.

'You mean it was—as you said—all a g-game? And now it's over. I disappointed you?' Her lips trembled and there was the suspicion of tears on her lashes, but she did her best to keep control. She did not want him knowing how upset she really was.

'Yes, you disappointed me,' he agreed, his stony voice lashing her cruelly.

'And I bet you turned to Riva for comfort?' The words were out before she could stop them.

He eyed her coldly. 'Yes, I saw Riva. Now find your pencil and let's get down to work.'

The lump in Hannah's throat was too big to swallow and her stupid tears kept spilling over on to the pad. She was glad Jordan did not look at her—he would most certainly have sneered, and on top of his contempt it was more than she could handle.

He stood up immediately he had finished. 'I'd like those done today,' he told her curtly.

'But it will take me hours,' she protested. 'I won't be finished before Danny goes to bed. I must spend some time with him.'

'Then I suggest you get on with them instead of arguing,' he rasped. 'And don't forget to deliver those other letters. I want the tenants to have them today.'

He could have taken them himself, she thought uncharitably as he left the office. What was wrong with that? He had reverted to the impossible boss; he was going to be difficult to handle. But she had coped before, so she would again, she told herself stoically. All she had to do was stand up to him.

This was easier said than done. Now that she had been to bed with him every one of her layers of defence had been stripped away: he had seen her totally vulnerable, every raw nerve exposed and taken and used—and now she was discarded like an empty paper bag.

Only last night she had envisaged a lifetime together, in fact Jordan had spoken about it himself, but now there was nothing. He would keep her here to do the job he had brought her to do, but once everything was running to his satisfaction and Drew took over—what then? Would she be out of a home and out of a job? Or would he keep her tied to his side and make her suffer? The thought did not bear thinking about.

It was a long time before she gathered her wits sufficiently to concentrate on typing his letters, and even then she did them automatically without taking anything in. But at length they were finished. It was half-past six. Daniel would have eaten but not be in bed. He could walk with her to take those other letters. His company and fresh air were what she needed right now.

But when she went in search of her son he was nowhere in sight. Nor was Jordan. She found Mrs Savill in the kitchen preparing their dinner, and the woman told her that they had gone out together. 'Something about a pony,' she added.

Hannah was furious. Jordan had gone to buy Danny his pony without saying anything to her? How could he do that? 'Where exactly have they gone?' she asked.

'Search me,' shrugged the older woman.

'When did they go?'

'Straight after your son finished his tea.'

'And you've no idea where?'

'I'm sorry, Mrs Quest, he didn't say.'

'I wish he'd told me,' said Hannah, trying without much luck to control her temper. 'I would have liked to go with them.'

Mrs Savill sympathised. 'Whenever Mr Quest makes up his mind he does things straight away.'

Hannah agreed. It had been an equally sudden decision when Jordan had asked her to marry him.

There was no sense in hanging around waiting for them to come back. Armed with the letters, she set off briskly for the cottages. She had delivered the last one and was rounding the corner by the farmhouse when suddenly Daniel came galloping towards her on a pony that was far too big for him, a look of abject terror on his face.

Hannah did what most mothers would do instinctively: she caught hold of the pony's reins as he shot past her and hung on, using all her strength to bring him to a halt. But it was not enough. The pony was also frightened, and now Hannah was being dragged along as well. When he headed for a narrow gateway she knew there wasn't room for both of them, but neither was there time to let go!

CHAPTER ELEVEN

THE old wooden gatepost tore through Hannah's clothes
to her skin, but she was oblivious to the pain, thinking
only of her son. Miraculously the pony halted, virtually
skidding to halt when confronted by both Jordan and
the burly farmer. Hannah could not think what Jordan
was doing here in this yard when he should have been
with Daniel, but this was no time to ask questions.

She felt bruised all over and was trembling so much
she could hardly stand, but she lifted her arms up to
Daniel, who had tears streaming down his face and was
still hanging on to the pony's mane like grim death.

Jordan's strong arms reached Daniel before hers,
lifting him easily, stooping down beside him as he stood
him on the ground. 'Are you all right, little man? That
was some ride!' There was actually admiration on his
face.

Hannah could not believe it. *'Some ride!'* she stormed.
'He could have been killed! You had no right letting him
go off alone like that. He——'

'Hannah, calm down,' Jordan said quietly, his eyes
skimming over her own dishevelled state. 'We'll talk
about it later. Let me handle Daniel. The wrong words
now and you'll have him frightened of horses for life.'

She clenched her teeth and glared, and keeping quiet
was the most difficult thing she had ever done. Jordan
spoke softly and encouragingly to Daniel, and because
Jordan was his hero Danny listened attentively and within
minutes he was smiling and saying proudly to Hannah,

'I was pretending to be a cowboy, Mummy, you needn't have tried to stop me. I was going fast on purpose.'

Hannah glanced coldly at Jordan over the top of his head and then hugged her son to her. 'It was very clever of you, Danny—I didn't realise. But I think we ought to go home now and get cleaned up, don't you?' Every bone in her body ached; surely some of them must be broken?

'OK,' he agreed eagerly. 'Can I have a piggyback, Dad?'

'Of course, son,' and to the farmer, 'Will you see to Captain, Jim?'

'Sure will. You look after the child—and Mrs Quest. She looks as though she's in need of some tender loving care as well.' The farmer winked at Hannah as he spoke and she knew he was hinting at the fact that they were newlyweds.

Jordan turned to Hannah and there was concern in his eyes as he looked at her, but she knew he did not really care, that this display of sympathy was for the farmer's benefit alone. 'Can you manage to walk?' he asked softly, 'or shall I fetch the car?'

Her lips were tight. 'I'll walk.' But it was an effort to put one foot in front of the other and she did not know which part of her hurt most. When they got to the house she sent Daniel up to his room and asked Jordan if he would like to supervise his bath and put him to bed. She knew he would agree, he loved doing anything for her son. They had built up a tremendous rapport over the short time they had known each other.

'I think you're the one I should be looking after,' he said firmly. 'You shouldn't have tried to stop Captain, you could have got yourself killed.'

'And my son could have been killed if I hadn't!' she retorted furiously.

'I don't think so.' His brown eyes were intent on hers. 'Captain was on his way back to the stable. He knew exactly where he was going.'

'Danny didn't know that, and neither did I. Danny was frightened out of his wits!'

'Mention that in front of him and I'll screw your neck,' Jordan muttered fiercely. 'You'll undo all the good I've done. As far as he's concerned it was nothing more than an exciting adventure.'

'You had no right letting him out alone on that pony in the first place,' she accused, wondering why, in the heat of this argument, when it was her son's life they were discussing, she still felt his dangerous sexual power. It seemed he had only to look at her and she went to pieces. Her body wasn't her own any more.

'It was Daniel's suggestion,' he told her. 'He assured me he could ride, I watched him go round the yard a few times, and Captain is the mildest of all the ponies. I wouldn't have let Daniel go on him unsupervised otherwise.'

'He wasn't very placid when I saw him.'

'Yes, I know.' He frowned thoughtfully. 'I don't understand it. Something must have happened to scare him, but I didn't think it wise to question Daniel today. I shall get to the bottom of it, though, don't worry, and Daniel won't go on Captain again unless I'm with him.'

Hannah, too weary to stand any longer, turned away and headed up the stairs. 'Make sure you do,' she said. 'My son is very precious to me.'

'You think he's not to me too?' Jordan asked softly over her shoulder.

'Oh, I think you like him all right,' she agreed, 'but there are no blood ties. If anything happened to Danny I'd kill myself.'

'That's silly talk, Hannah.'

'Is it?' she snapped. 'Not having the capacity to fall in love, you wouldn't know what it's like. Losing Roger was like a death sentence, but if Danny went as well life definitely wouldn't be worth living.'

'Of course—Roger. I forgot for one moment that he was the love of your life.' The contempt was back. 'I doubt if you'll ever make any attempt to let anyone take his place. I seem to have got myself into a no-win situation.'

Now should have been the time for her to tell him that Roger had already taken second place, that after last night she had discovered a love so deep and meaningful that she wondered why she had ever called what it was she felt for Roger love. But Jordan was in no mood to listen; it would do no good. He quite possibly despised her for giving herself so freely to him last night. Certainly something had happened, though she doubted if she would ever find out exactly what thoughts had gone through his mind.

At Daniel's door he stopped, asking tersely, 'Are you sure you're in a fit state to bathe yourself?'

Hannah nodded, but would have said yes even if she were dying. It would have been more than flesh and blood could stand to have him touch her. But once alone in the room her legs felt as though they would no longer hold her weight, and she staggered to the bed. There were aches in her heart as well as her body, and she wondered how long she would be able to put up with Jordan treating her like this.

He had talked about a no-win situation, but she felt as though she was in one herself. There was no future with him, and yet she hadn't the financial independence to go elsewhere. As she was his wife he did not pay her a salary, and although he had mentioned opening her a bank account he had done nothing about it yet. In any case, she wouldn't touch a penny of his money; the last thing she wanted was to be indebted to him.

When the door opened and Jordan came in, his shirt sleeves rolled up, his hair damp and curly after being in the bathroom with Daniel, Hannah realised that she had lain there longer than she intended. He frowned harshly when he saw her struggling to sit up. 'What are you doing?' he demanded.

Hannah winced as she moved and he was at her side instantly. 'Here, let me.' A hand for her to hold on to, a steadying arm about her waist—and *frissons* of feeling running through her!

'Why didn't you tell me you were hurt this badly?' he demanded, as she found it difficult to stand.

'I was more interested in Daniel than myself. It's just a few bruises—it's nothing. Once I've had a bath I'll feel better.'

'You need more than a bath. I'd say you need medical attention,' he snorted. 'First of all, let's get rid of these clothes.'

He was so expert that it was obviously not the first time he had undressed a woman, but Hannah doubted whether it had been done so clinically before. She wished she had the strength to object.

When her clothes lay in a pile on the floor his eyes sought each graze and bruise, his lips pursed as he saw the extent of her injuries. 'My God, Hannah, how did all this happen?' he demanded.

'You know very well how it happened,' she told him fiercely, wishing she could stem the rising tide of emotion that his touch evoked. 'I was trying to stop the pony and he dragged me along, and I hurt my shoulders when he charged through the gate.'

'I'll say you hurt your shoulders!' he rasped. 'There's hardly any skin left on them!'

Hannah felt sure he was exaggerating.

'I'll run you a warm bath and clean your wounds, then we'll see whether you need a doctor.'

He was briskly efficient, and as she stepped, with his help, into the water he had mildly disinfected, Hannah could not help musing on the difference in him between now and last night. If he had still been in the same mood he would have turned this whole affair into a game of love. His actions would have been entirely sensual as he disrobed her, he would touched and excited, stroked and aroused, and she would have forgotten all about her aches and pains. Instead his lips were tight, his actions detached, and she could have been his worst enemy for all the interest he showed.

The water stung when she first slid in, but within seconds it soothed and calmed. Jordan remained looking down at her, his eyes totally expressionless. She actually found it difficult to understand how he could be so hot-blooded one moment and so coldly indifferent the next. As far as she was concerned you either cared for a person or you didn't. If you loved them you loved them to distraction, and your moods were no different one day to the next. But she kept forgetting, Jordan did not love her. There were no emotions at all in his cold soul, his heart was a swinging brick, and it was clear now why he had never married. No girl in her right mind would put up with someone whose moods were as changeable as Jordan's.

She closed her eyes for a moment to try and shut him out, but opened them quickly when she heard him messing about in the water. He had a face-flannel in his hands and was ready to wash her as he'd washed Daniel earlier. One part of her wanted to scream out in protest, but the other more dominant part, her sensual part, let him get on with it. This would probably be the last time he touched her, and even though it was crazy loving him when he was so dispassionate, she hadn't the will-power to deny her needs.

First he wiped over her face, paying particular attention to the smudges of mascara beneath her eyes. Hannah found herself trembling beneath his touch and hoped he would think it was all connected to her ordeal. He was so close she could see the brown flecks in his irises, and she wanted to reach out and touch, but knew she did not dare.

Discarding the flannel and using his hands instead, he washed her arms, lifting each up in turn, then her legs and feet, mindful of her bruised knees. His touch was gentle and caring, and had it not been for his lack of emotion Hannah would have said he was enjoying it. He was particularly careful when he washed her back, and quite brief, but when his hands moved to soap her breasts it seemed that he deliberately slowed his movements. Hannah felt the room begin to spin and closed her eyes so that she would not see those tanned, long-fingered hands performing so intimate a task.

Every one of her pulses throbbed, every part of her clamoured for something more than this cool, detached performance. When she could stand the assault no longer, when outrage began to take the place of enjoyment, she pushed him roughly away. 'I think that's enough,' she said quickly.

His smile was a sneer. 'I wondered when you were going to stop me. For all your protests about still being faithful to your—to Roger—you seem to find a great deal of pleasure in my touching you.'

'That's a lie,' she snapped. 'You were deliberately taking advantage.'

'Was I taking advantage last night too? Did I get it wrong? Were you not as willing as I thought?' he asked savagely. 'No, don't answer, I don't want to hear any more of your lies. Let's get you out of here.'

She used his arm as a lever and allowed him to pat her sore shoulders dry, but then she took the towel from him and ordered him out. His lips quirked at her belated prudery. 'Give me a call when you're finished and I'll put some ointment on your wounds. They're not as bad as I first thought, but you sure as hell are going to be stiff and sore in the morning.'

It came as a relief when Jordan declared, later that evening, that he was going to sleep in one of the other rooms. 'I don't want to knock you accidentally,' he explained, but Hannah felt sure it was because of whatever had happened to poison his mind towards her.

Nevertheless she was glad he was moving out. She'd had the uneasy feeling all day that despite his attitude he would have no compunction about using her in bed. And that would have been unbearable.

That night was the most uncomfortable Hannah had ever spent. In whichever position she lay it hurt, and she was up far earlier than usual, washing and dressing, wincing as the soft material of her blouse chafed against the grazes. In the end she took the blouse off and put on a strapless sun-top. It was a splendid July day, warm even at this hour, and as Daniel was not yet awake she went outside to walk by the moat.

It was a pity, she felt, that the serenity out here was not reflected indoors. There was far too much tension between her and Jordan for her ever to be happy. It really had been a fatal mistake thinking that marriage to a man of his type would work. The fact that he was still single at the age of thirty-five should have told her something.

She paused by a stone bench and sat down, gazing with troubled eyes at the limpid water, listening to the song of a blackbird. There were no other sounds except for the occasional faint low of a cow—and wasn't that the drumming hoofs of a galloping horse? She shaded her eyes and in the distance saw a horse and rider come into sight, but it was not until they got much closer that she saw it was Jordan on a massive black stallion—and her foolish heart trembled in response.

He did not see her until he reined the horse to a halt the other side of the moat, and by this time her pulses had joined in the clamour. Was there to be no end to her torment? wondered Hannah. Why couldn't she treat him with the same indifference as he was handing out? He came over the bridge and trotted up to her, looking down from his great height.

The horse was beautiful, smooth and glossy, powerful muscles rippling, feet prancing. Jordan handled him superbly. There was no doubt who was the master. Dressed in black also, he and the horse made an impressive team, and had it been any other day than a brilliant summer morning they could have looked sinister.

Jordan's eyes flicked casually over her. Even they looked totally black in this thin morning air. 'This is a surprise. Do I take it you didn't sleep well?'

'What did you expect?' she asked bitterly, standing up in an attempt to reduce some of the space between them. But it was more than a couple of yards, it was a whole world. There had been the faintest hope in her heart that he might have changed towards her, that he might have reverted to the loving man he had been two nights ago. It had been a futile thought. His eyes held the obsidian hardness of volcanic rock.

'Your war wounds troubled you?'

The hint of humour surprised her. 'You can say that again!'

He slid down off the horse. 'Let me see.'

As his hands touched her shoulders fresh tremors of awareness shot through her. She wanted to turn and press herself into him, to feel the exciting hardness of his body once again. It was an effort to submit to his inspection without turning a hair—and he seemed to take an awfully long time about it.

'It looks as though the sheets have rubbed your grazes,' he told her needlessly. 'You're very wise to wear something like this today. Better than a dressing, because the air will help heal them.'

His fingers remained on the tops of her bare shoulders in a sensual caress, or was it all in her mind? Was it wishful thinking because that was what she wanted to feel? She moved away, casually so that he would not know it was because she could no longer stand him touching her. It was the first time she had ever seen him in jodhpurs. Both they and the fine cashmere sweater fitted him like a second skin, accentuating every powerful muscle.

A brief flare of anger lit his eyes, and she knew he had not mistaken her movement for anything other than what it was. 'I trust,' he said coldly, 'that you'll be up to working today?'

Her chin lifted. 'But of course. It will take more than a little thing like this to stop me.'

'Good,' he growled, putting his foot in the stirrup and swinging himself back up on the magnificent horse. 'I'll see you later.' He touched his hat in a mock salute and in moments horse and rider were once again mere figures in the distance.

Hannah watched until he was out of sight before she headed back to the house. Judging by the mood he was in she had a difficult day in front of her—but she did not realise exactly how difficult until their first visitor arrived, in the form of Jordan's mother.

Halfway through the morning, unannounced, she swept imperiously into the estate office. She took in at a glance the tense atmosphere, and a faintly satisfied smile curved her thin lips. 'I've come to see how things are going, Jordan,' she announced. To all intents and purposes she was referring to the estate, but Hannah knew she meant nothing of the sort. And they had just given her the proof she needed that their marriage was not working out!

'Things are going very well, Mother, thank you,' replied Jordan, smiling easily. 'We've sorted out the mess Henderson made and now it's all systems go. Would you like a cup of coffee?' When she nodded he said to Hannah, 'Would you mind, darling, going and telling Mrs Savill?'

Darling! So the façade was being played for his mother's benefit? Hannah could not see why, because she would find out soon enough that they were living a sham—if indeed they lived together for very long. It seemed a pointless exercise, but if that was what Jordan wanted then she would go along with it. She gave him one of her most dazzling smiles as she got up.

'Goodness me, what have you done to your back?' asked Mrs Quest in shocked horror. 'Jordan?'

'It's nothing to worry about, Mother. Hannah had an accident with a horse, that's all.'

Still she frowned. 'It looks pretty horrific to me. Have you been to the doctor's, Hannah?'

It was the first time she had spoken directly to Hannah, and it took her by surprise. 'I don't think that's necessary. Jordan's looking after me very well, aren't you, my sweet?'

The briefest flicker of his eyes at her endearment. 'Mmm, yes, I'm giving her every ounce of loving care that she deserves.'

Which was nil, thought Hannah tightly, but she kept the smile pinned to her lips as she left the office.

Mrs Quest stayed for lunch. On the surface she was charming and polite, though she made sure Riva was mentioned in the conversation, and by the time she left Hannah's face muscles felt stiff from forcing too many smiles, both for her benefit and Jordan's.

'I don't know why we bothered,' she said when they were alone. 'Your mother knew there was something wrong. She sensed it the moment she walked into the office.'

'My mother is not going to have the satisfaction of knowing that I've made a mistake,' he growled murderously. 'You're stuck with me for the rest of your life, whether you like it or not.'

'You'd stay with me for *her* sake?' asked Hannah, eyes incredulous.

'Not particularly, but mine, yes,' he snarled.

She shook her head in total disbelief. 'I suppose what you're trying to say is that you'll keep up a pretence of a happy marriage but you'll have no compunction about going to bed with Riva?' How she wished she could afford to leave him!

He eyed her with brutal coldness. 'If you drive me to it, then yes, I suppose it could happen,' he agreed.

Hannah was even more sure it could happen when Mrs Savill announced later that afternoon that a Miss Riva March was waiting to see Mr Quest.

Letting her breath out on a sigh of anger and resentment, Hannah said coolly, 'It's a little early, but I'll go and fetch Daniel. In that way you'll be able to have a cosy tête-à-tête without worrying about me.'

'If that's what you want,' Jordan answered, his brown eyes fiercely narrowed. 'I'm more than willing to fetch Daniel, you know that.'

'And leave me here with Riva?' she asked scornfully. 'No, thanks. I'll see you later. Don't worry if I don't come straight back. I might take Daniel for a walk.'

She met Riva as she left the office. The blonde girl eyed her warily but defiantly, and immediately Hannah's hackles rose. She smiled with all the confidence of a woman in love, which wasn't difficult considering how she felt. 'You won't be able to tempt my husband away from the straight and narrow,' she purred softly, marvelling how seductive she was able to make her voice sound. 'He was just saying that marrying me was the best thing that ever happened to him. We're so blissfully happy.'

At that moment Jordan came to the door, and Hannah's heart sank as she realised he had heard every word. But she continued to smile bravely and let her love shine in her eyes. 'Isn't that true, darling,' she said to him, touching his arm and reaching up to press a light kiss to his mouth.

'Absolutely, my precious.' His hand curved around the back of her neck, and the kiss became a force to be contended with, flaring inside Hannah like a firework on Bonfire Night. She actually felt sorry for Riva having to witness this display of unbridled passion, though she doubted whether the other girl would have felt any such emotion if the roles were reversed.

Hannah gave her all, knowing it would be one of only a very few occasions when Jordan would kiss her, and determined to enjoy every second of it.

'Run along now, my love,' he muttered thickly, dragging his mouth away from hers as if with reluctance. 'And hurry back—I'll miss you.'

If only she could believe him! Hannah left the house with a wildly beating heart but unhappiness in her mind.

Daniel was surprised to see her instead of Jordan, but accepted the fact that his new father had a visitor, and was quite happy to go walking round the estate instead of heading straight home.

When they did finally get back to the Hall Riva had gone and Jordan was waiting for them. He scooped Daniel up in his arms and whirled him around, the two of them laughing joyfully together. A pang of jealousy shot through Hannah. Life would have been perfect if Jordan loved her too.

'How do you feel about getting changed and going riding again?' Jordan asked Daniel as he put him down.

Hannah glanced sharply both at her husband and son. She was not sure that it was such a good idea after his fright yesterday.

But Daniel nodded eagerly. 'Yes, please. I've told everyone at school about my pony.' He seemed to have settled in remarkably well after his bad start.

'I'll come and watch you,' she said.

But Jordan had other ideas. 'I've left some accounts for you to go through,' he told her sharply. 'There are several outstanding bills that need strong letters, and also cheques to be made out.'

'But why should I work when you've finished?' she wanted to know.

'You've just had over an hour off, Hannah.'

'While you were talking to Riva,' she accused.

'Riva stayed no more than a few minutes,' he told her, 'and, for your peace of mind, I shan't be seeing her again.'

He watched closely for her reaction, but Hannah was growing adept at keeping a guard over her feelings and she merely shrugged, as if to say, I'll believe that if it happens.

While they were talking Daniel had rushed upstairs to get changed, and now he came down again and tugged eagerly at Jordan's arm. 'Let's go!' And casually, 'Are you coming, Mummy?'

When she shook her head he did not seem in the least disappointed. He really enjoyed the time he spent alone with Jordan, and if Hannah were to be totally honest, Jordan was handling her son much better than Roger ever had. It was an unkind thought, she knew, but it was true.

By the time she had finished the accounts they were back, Daniel chattering ceaselessly about Captain, at the same time complaining how hungry he was. 'Your bath first, I think,' she said. 'Mrs Savill won't be very pleased if you sit at the table smelling of horses.'

'Can Dad come with me?' he asked eagerly.

Before she could say anything Jordan shook his head. 'It's your mother's turn. She'll be upset if I do everything for you.'

'Will you, Mummy?' asked Daniel curiously.

Hannah nodded, Jordan's understanding bringing a lump to her throat. He was proving to be a perfect father, why couldn't he be a perfect husband? Why couldn't he love her as she loved him? With every hour they spent together her love grew deeper, and yet it was so futile—this was what hurt most.

Later, when Daniel was in bed and they were eating their dinner, Hannah having changed into a soft lawn dress that did not rub her wounds, Jordan told her that he had found out what had caused Captain to bolt.

'It was nothing more than a bin liner, a black plastic dustbin liner. It had caught in the lower branches of a tree and was flapping in the wind,' he explained. 'I didn't know this, but apparently some youths frightened him by putting a plastic bag over his head when he was a few months old.'

'Causing him to be frightened of plastic bags ever since,' said Hannah, understanding now in her eyes. 'How was Danny on him today?'

'Pretty cocksure,' grinned Jordan. 'He's a born rider, believe me.' He sounded as proud as if Daniel were his own son. 'He did a lot of riding when you lived on the farm, did he?'

'Not really,' she said. 'Roger took him occasionally, but he was always so busy, he worked long hours and came home dreadfully tired and never had time for Dan——' She broke off, realising how disloyal that sounded.

Jordan's well-marked brows rose. This was the first hint she had given him that Roger was anything but perfect. 'How about you? Did he neglect you the same as it appears he did Daniel?' His tone was suddenly sharp, intentness in his eyes as he waited for her answer.

'I was happy with Roger,' she defended at length, unwilling to tell him that there were too many nights when he had fallen into bed and dropped straight off to sleep. And it was true, she had been happy—very happy. It was only since she'd met Jordan that she had discovered a whole new world of emotions. But what she'd never had she had never missed, so it would have been wrong of her to say that she hadn't been happy.

'How happy?' he wanted to know, his tone curt.

'How can you measure happiness?' she countered.

'There are varying degrees, believe me,' he answered coldly. 'Total happiness is when a couple are compatible in every single way. Do you get my meaning?'

Hannah's throat and cheeks flushed.

'For instance, what sort of a lover was he?' Jordan pursued.

'I don't think that's any of your business,' she gasped.

'Was he as good as me?'

'There's no comparison,' she retorted, knowing he would interpret it wrongly.

His eyes narrowed until all she could see was glittering jet. 'Was that why you called out for him the other night? I didn't satisfy you, was that it?'

Hannah stilled and frowned. 'What are you talking about?'

'As if you don't know!' he spat. 'Do you deny that you were thinking about him? That he mentally replaced me in your arms? Was it him all along you were thinking of when you made love to me? What the hell do you think I felt like when you lay in my arms afterwards and called out his name?'

'Oh, Jordan!' exclaimed Hannah at once. 'I was dreaming, that's all. I dreamt about Roger and I told him about you. He was so happy for me. He didn't like to think of me being alone, he said. If I mentioned his name I wasn't aware of it.' And because she felt that this was a moment for total honesty she added quietly, 'Roger has never made love to me as you did. It was the most wonderful night of my life.' Her cheeks coloured pink as she made the confession.

'I wish I could believe that, Hannah.' His eyes continued to stab her with icicles of frozen dislike.

She shook her head furiously. 'Believe what you like, but it's true. I've had enough of this conversation, I'm going out for some fresh air.' It had been hard enough making the confession, but for Jordan to disbelieve her! It was more than she could bear.

An iron hand gripped her wrist as she rushed past his chair. 'If it was such a wonderful experience, Hannah, why have you been rejecting me ever since? Why have you moved away every time I get near you? Why do I get the impression that I'm repulsive to you?'

Hannah was blinded by a haze of helplessness. Did she tell him the truth or lie through her teeth? Her whole body began to shake, and he thrust her away from him in despair. 'If you're really so put off by me, Hannah, then you're free to go.'

'I don't want to go,' she whispered painfully.

'You mean you want to stay, even though you don't love me nor ever will?' he asked derisively.

She swallowed hard and in a voice that was choked with emotion and almost too quiet for him to hear, she said, 'I do love you, Jordan—that's the trouble.'

The quick frown that knitted his brows told her that he had had no difficulty in hearing her words. 'You— love me? You honestly love me, is that what you're saying?'

She nodded.

'You no longer love Roger?' he asked huskily.

'I've learned to let go.'

He groaned and his head fell down into his hands.

Hannah did not know what to make of this. His shoulders were heaving and it was as though he were crying—but why should he? Why should her confession have such a devastating effect? 'Jordan?' She touched his shoulder tentatively and felt him flinch, and would have backed away if the next second he hadn't swung upright and crushed her against him.

She thought every bone in her body was going to snap. She felt shudder after shudder wash through him until finally, his voice thick with emotion, he said, 'This is the happiest day of my life! Oh, Hannah, my dearest Hannah, you don't know what this means to me!'

With trembling fingers she held his head against her wildly beating breast, stroked the thickness of his hair and waited.

'I've always thought of love as being a word that's used too loosely—you know that, Hannah. But whatever its guise I've never believed in it. Until this moment.'

'You believe that I love you?' she asked faintly.

'I believe you.'

'I—I love you—even more than I loved Roger,' she whispered achingly and bravely.

'Oh, God, Hannah, I don't deserve this.'

'I have enough love for the two of us if you'll just let me into your life.' Her lips trembled, tears welling and spilling. 'I don't care if you don't love me. It doesn't matter, just as long as you'll be my friend and make love to me now and then.'

'But it does matter,' he interjected fiercely. 'It matters where you're concerned. You're not Riva, or any other girl I've been out with. You're the spunky girl who faced up to me in the office and has been sparring with me ever since. You're brave and beautiful and a caring, loving mother and very loyal to Roger—and oh, darling, I love you—if love's the word you want, then yes, I love you so much.'

Hannah could not believe that she was hearing him correctly. Jordan loved her! The man who had sworn never to fall in love was now saying that she meant more to him than anyone else in the world. 'I can't believe it,' she whispered.

'It's true, my precious. You've achieved the impossible. You've brought me, the invincible Jordan Quest, down to my knees. I worship every hair of your head. I love you, I love Daniel, and I shall love every one of our children.'

Hannah's cheeks coloured becomingly, and when his mouth sought hers she surrendered. It was a long time before either of them stirred again.

'Did you love me when you asked me to marry you?' she asked wonderingly.

'I knew I wanted you more than anyone else. I knew I never wanted to let you go. But you were still emotionally tied to Roger, that was the trouble. I knew I had a battle on my hands, but I thought I'd got over the first hurdle when you let me make love to you. It nearly killed me when I heard you calling out for Roger so shortly afterwards.'

'I'm sorry about that,' she whispered, tracing the strong lines of his face with a trembling finger. Everything had happened so quickly it was unbelievable. 'But did you have to turn to Riva? God, that hurt, the thought of you with her after me.'

'No, my darling, no,' Jordan assured her gently, 'don't ever think that. I haven't touched Riva in that way since I met you. I used her, yes, to make you jealous—I couldn't stand your indifference, but there hasn't been anything between us for a long, long time.' He touched her finger with his tongue as it passed over his lips. 'Life's going to take on a whole new meaning, Hannah. We'll work and play and love together. The only time we might have any difficulties is with Daniel when we've finished here and turn it over to Drew. My house at Hunter's Hill isn't on quite the same scale.'

'You could sell it and buy this from Drew,' she suggested tentatively. 'I can't really see him ever running this estate. With the money he'd be a rich man, he could buy a small house somewhere and——'

'And spend the rest of it before he was thirty,' snorted Jordan. 'I don't think that's a very good idea, but never mind, we'll think of something. The important thing is that we've discovered our love for each other.' His mouth closed over hers once again. 'Oh, Hannah, my love,' he muttered, 'don't ever leave me. Love me for ever.'

'I will, I will,' she breathed. 'I promise.' Her love for this man was so much stronger than anything she had felt for Roger. Not that she would ever say anything against him. Roger had loved her in his own way and she had loved him, but love this second time around was different. It was on a higher level, so much more physical and emotional. Life would be one constant round of excitement and fulfilment.

'What are you thinking, my love?'

She smiled. 'That I'd like to go to bed with you, Mr Quest.'

'That, Mrs Quest,' he said softly, 'is something that can be very easily arranged.' Mindful of her sore shoulders, he picked her up in his arms and carried her upstairs.

Hi,

Italy, as always, is a model's paradise. But I'm tired of the obligatory parties, the devouring eyes. Particularly those of Nicolo Sabatini, who seems to think I should be for his eyes only.

Love, Caroline

Take 4 bestselling love stories FREE

Plus get a FREE surprise gift!

Special Limited-time Offer

Mail to Harlequin Reader Service®

3010 Walden Avenue
P.O. Box 1867
Buffalo, N.Y. 14269-1867

YES! Please send me 4 free Harlequin Presents® novels and my free surprise gift. Then send me 6 brand-new novels every month, which I will receive months before they appear in bookstores. Bill me at the low price of $2.44 each plus 25¢ delivery and applicable sales tax, if any*. That's the complete price and—compared to the cover prices of $2.99 each—quite a bargain! I understand that accepting the books and gift places me under no obligation ever to buy any books. I can always return a shipment and cancel at any time. Even if I never buy another book from Harlequin, the 4 free books and the surprise gift are mine to keep forever.

106 BPA ANRH

Name _____ (PLEASE PRINT)

Address _____ Apt. No. _____

City _____ State _____ Zip _____

This offer is limited to one order per household and not valid to present Harlequin Presents® subscribers. *Terms and prices are subject to change without notice. Sales tax applicable in N.Y.

UPRES-94R   ©1990 Harlequin Enterprises Limited

This June, Harlequin invites you to a wedding of

Promised Brides

Celebrate the joy and romance of weddings past with PROMISED BRIDES—a collection of original historical short stories, written by three best-selling historical authors:

> *The Wedding of the Century*—MARY JO PUTNEY
> *Jesse's Wife*—KRISTIN JAMES
> *The Handfast*—JULIE TETEL

Three unforgettable heroines, three award-winning authors! PROMISED BRIDES is available in June wherever Harlequin Books are sold.

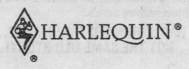

HARLEQUIN®

PB94